A THUG'S DEVOTION

J. L. ROSE

J. M. MCMILLON

GOOD2GO PUBLISHING

A THUG'S DEVOTION

Written by J. L. Rose and J. M. McMillons
Cover Design: Davida Baldwin
Typesetter: Mychea
ISBN: 9781947340121

Published 2017 by Good2Go Publishing
7311 W. Glass Lane • Laveen, AZ 85339
www.good2gopublishing.com
https://twitter.com/good2gobooks
G2G@good2gopublishing.com
www.facebook.com/good2gopublishing
www.instagram.com/good2gopublishing

DEDICATIONS

To my heavenly Father, I thank you each day for this blessing that you've given me and your undying love. Also to my fans, I love each of you because of your loyalty and your love for my work. I love each of you. We just getting started. Love!

~ J. L. Rose

I would like to dedicate this book to my wife and my heavenly Father, but a special thanks to my roommate, J.L. Rose, for allowing me to work with him on this book. Blessings!

~ J. M. McMillon

ACKNOWLEDGEMENTS

People, understand that just because I may not mention you in my books, it does not mean I do not hear and feel the love, because I do. I hear each of you and thank you. Now to name a few people. I got to show love to both my mom, Ludie A. Rose, and my pops, John L. Rose. I can never thank you two enough for all the two of you do for me. I love you to life. Also, much love to Mychea, author of *He Loves Me, He Loves You Not*. Ma, you is crazy fine with the pen game, and I hope I'm still your new favorite author, because you are definitely mine! Love and blessings.

~ J. L. Rose

To J. L. Rose, my wife and kids, and also to Good2Go Publishing. Thank you greatly.

~ J. M. McMillon

PROLOGUE

"Thank God!" Karinne cried with the roll of her eyes, once the school bell rang, ending the school day.

She was happy since it was Friday and the start of a three-day weekend, so she snatched up her bag and headed for the door, barely getting two feet away from the classroom when she heard her name called. Karinne turned back to see her girls, Gina and April, so she waited for them to catch up to her.

"Karinne, girl. You not gonna believe who was looking for you just now!" April told her best friend as the three of them headed toward the front of the school.

"Who?" Karinne asked as she pushed open the door and exited the front entrance to her senior high school.

"Jason Hensen, girl!" both April and Gina said together, smiling at Karinne.

Karinne sucked her teeth knowing exactly who her girls were talking about, but she was truly not impressed with him. So Karinne changed the subject as she walked up to her Lexus GS 350.

"Is we going to this party tonight at Kelly and Kim's house?"

"Hell yeah!" April yelled as she opened the front passenger door to the Lexus.

Once all three girls were inside the car and Karinne was backing out of her parking space and out of the lot, she listened to April talking about what she heard about the party that was supposed to be going on that night. She lost focus on what April was saying when she noticed the light-skinned guy she recognized who had just moved into the house next door to her and her mother and stepfather.

"Damn, bitch!" April said, noting the way Karinne was staring at the light-skinned young man with a lot of hair up in a ponytail.

"Karinne, you know Victor?" Gina asked, also noticing the guy.

"What's his name?" Karinne asked, looking back at Gina through the rearview mirror.

"It's Victor McKnight!" Gina told her girl. "He's in my sixth-period class."

"Anyway!" April began. "Karinne, stop at Mr. Ed's store on the corner. I'm hungry."

Karinne did as April had asked, and turned her Lexus into the corner store parking lot at the end of the street from the school. After she parked the car, all three young women got out and stepped into the store.

Karinne walked toward the refrigerators in the back of the store and grabbed a sweet tea. She then picked up a bag of Doritos and was just turning to head back up to the counter only to pause a brief moment as the same guy who Gina had introduced as Victor was now turning down the same aisle. She caught and held his cat-like light-hazel-brown eyes and received a nod in return as he passed her.

Karinne was surprised at how cute Victor actually looked up

close, and she realized he looked mixed with something. She then met up with Gina and April at the counter.

"Girl, you ready?" April asked, since she and Gina were already ready to leave.

After Karinne paid for her items, she glanced back to see where Victor was. She then caught sight of him as he stepped up to the counter.

"Here comes the bullshit!" April announced, drawing both Gina's and Karinne's attention to the Ford Tahoe that was parking right beside the Lexus. "Here comes J. Prince and his stupid-ass boys with their shit!"

Karinne walked to her car and ignored J. Prince, even after he called to her once he hopped out of his Tahoe. As she stepped up to unlock her car door, J. Prince rushed up on her and pushed the car door back shut.

"Karinne, what's up, baby?" J. Prince asked as he got all up on Karinne. "You thought about what I said?"

"Ain't nothing to think about, Josophe!" she told him, using his real name, which caused both her girls to laugh. "I already told you we ain't got nothing to talk about, and I don't want you. Period!"

"Karinne, why you gotta—"

"Bye, boy!" Karinne interrupted, pushing J. Prince out of the way and reopening the car door, only for him to push the door back shut.

"Nigga! What the fuck wrong with you? Don't be slamming my door, and why the fuck is you still in my face begging?" she went off.

"Begging?" J. Prince yelled. "Bitch, who begging your dick-sucking ass? I'm just trying to get my dick wet!"

"Fuck you, nigga, with your punk ass! Move!" Karinne screamed, pushing him out of the way again, only for J. Prince to shove her up against the car and get in her face.

However, he was instantly snatched off and thrown to the side so hard that he fell into the side of his Tahoe.

"What the!" J. Prince yelled.

J. Prince rushed back up onto the person who placed his hands on him, only to pull to a quick stop as he came face-to-face with the light-skinned young man who stared him straight in the face.

"We got a problem?" Victor asked as he maintained eye contact with J. Prince. "My advice is you get back inside your Tahoe and leave."

"Or what?" one of J. Prince's four homeboys stated, making the mistake of approaching the light-skinned guy.

The homeboy never noticed the Yoo-hoo bottle that was gripped tightly in Victor's hand, until it was too late and smashed across the side of his face. Victor barely looked down at the would-be hero who was knocked out on the ground.

"Do we have a problem?" Victor asked as he looked over at J.

Prince.

"No, naw, man!" J. Prince got out as he quickly backed up with both hands in the air and got back into his Tahoe.

Victor watched the Tahoe as it drove away, and then he turned around and started walking away until he heard his name called out.

"Victor!"

He stopped and looked back at the female who he recognized as his next-door neighbor of where his parents had just moved.

"Yeah!"

"Ummm. Thank you!" Karinne replied as she stared at him with nothing more to say.

Nodding his head, he turned and walked off, leaving Karinne and her girls at the store.

ONE

Four hours later . . .

DONAVON PULLED UP IN front of his daughter's mother's house and saw three cars parked outside. Donavon King then picked up his cell phone from the center console and pulled up his daughter's number and called her. He sat and listened to the line ring twice before she answered.

"Hello!"

"I'm outside," Donavon told his daughter as he turned down Jay-Z's "Nickels and Dimes" that was playing throughout his Mercedes-Benz G63.

After hanging up the phone after Karinne said she'd be right out, he sat waiting a few minutes, when he saw the front door open and his sixteen-year-old daughter rush out of the house. He also noticed her mother standing at the front door watching her leave.

"Hi, Daddy!" Karinne said happily as she climbed into her father's G-Wagen Benz. She then leaned over and hugged him around his neck and kissed his cheek. "What's up?"

"I just stopped by to see how you was doing," Donavon told his daughter. "Everything good, baby girl?"

"Yes, Daddy. I'm doing fine."

"You sure?"

"Yes!"

"So what's this I hear you had a little problem today at old man Ed's store?" Donavon asked, seeing the surprised look that appeared on her face. "So do I need to ask again how you doing, Karinne?"

"Daddy, it's nothing!" she told her father. "This guy I kind of know took care of J. Prince and his boys."

"Yeah, I heard!" Donavon interrupted. "Some young light-skinned kid bust some kid across the head about you. Who was he?"

"Just this guy, Daddy."

"Who, Karinne?"

Karinne sighed and then looked over at the blue and white house next door. She was just about to answer her father's question when he spotted Victor standing and drinking something in the shadows of the driveway of the house.

"That him?" Donavon asked his daughter, noticing the young man standing in the shadows of his house.

"Yes, Daddy!" Karinne answered truthfully. "His name is Victor."

"Call him over," he told his daughter as he continued to watch the shadowed driveway, even as Karinne climbed from the Benz. When she called out to Victor, Donavon watched as the boy stepped into the light. "I'll be damned!"

Donovan recognized the young man who he remembered seeing

working at the car wash as well as cutting grass with Mr. Wallace's Lawn Service. Donovan heard his daughter tell the young hustler that he wanted to talk to the young man. Victor then walked over as Donavon climbed out of his G-Wagen and shut the door.

"What's good, youngin?" Donavon said as he walked around the front end of the Benz, stopping a few feet in front of the young hustler. "What's ya name, youngin?"

"I'm known as Knight, but the name's Victor McKnight," he responded. "What's up though? You wanna holla at me, old school?"

"I just wanted to thank you for what you did earlier for my baby girl," Donavon told him before asking, "Where you from, youngin? You Spanish or something?"

"Yeah!" Knight answered. "My pops is Jamaican, but my mom's Puerto Rican. My pops and me just moved here from Michigan."

"What part of Michigan?" Donavon asked him.

"Flint, Michigan," Knight replied as he looked over at Karinne as she loudly cleared her throat.

"Ummm, Daddy. I'm kind of supposed to be going out to a party tonight," Karinne informed her father.

"I'm holding you up?" he questioned jokingly before giving her a kiss on the forehead. "Call me if you need me. Here!"

Donavon dug out a phat knot from his pocket and gave his

daughter $300. He received another hug and kiss in return before Karinne took off back into the house. He then turned his attention back to the young hustler, only to catch the boy watching his daughter.

"So, how old is you, youngin?"

"You asked me that before when you came to the car wash some weeks ago," Knight told him. "You was driving an S-Class Benz thing."

"Oh, so you do remember me then, huh?" Donavon asked, noticing how sharp the young man was. "Why didn't you say anything before?"

"Not everything needs to be spoken," Knight told him, earning a small smile from Donavon.

"You're alright, youngin," Donavon said with a smile. "For a fifteen-year-old, you don't act or carry yourself like one, and you're taller than most boys your age. How tall are you?"

"I'm five foot, nine-and-a-half inches!"

Donavon nodded his head in approval of the young man and then asked, "Can you go for a ride or do your parents want you to stay in after a time?"

"My pops could care less what I do!" Knight answered. "Where we going?"

"For a ride," Donavon replied. "Come on, youngin!"

* * *

Knight left with Donavon as they just rode around and talked. Knight found himself doing most of the talking and opening up a little to Donavon. He wanted to know a little more about him since he caught good vibes from him. They soon pulled into an apartment complex called Oak Grove Apartments in North Miami.

"Come on, youngin!" Donavon said to Knight as he climbed from his G-Wagen.

As they walked from the parking lot and entered the complex, Donavon led Knight to an apartment door. Beyoncé's "Dangerously in Love" could be heard playing inside. Donavon pulled out a key from his keyring and unlocked the front door as the two walked inside.

"Donavon!" Melody happily cried out after noticing her man enter the apartment.

She hopped up from her seat and jumped over her girl, Faith, who sat on the floor in front of the sofa.

Donavon received a hug and a tongue kiss from one of his many women with whom he shared his time when he could. He slapped Melody on her soft and phat ass.

"Turn down the music some, woman!"

Melody did as she was asked. She walked over to her girl Tina and grabbed the remote and turned down the song. She then tossed the remote back over to Tina and turned back toward Donavon.

"Baby, what are you doing here? Who's that with you?"

"That's what I've been wanting to know!" Tina said, already eyeing up the sexy-as-hell, light-skinned boy who stood beside Donavon, with the pretty, long hair on his head. "Donavon, introduce us to your friend, boy!"

Donavon smiled as he cut his eyes over at the surprisingly calm and relaxed young man.

"Melody. Tina. Faith. This is my youngin, Knight," Donavon introduced.

"How you doing, Knight? It's good meeting you," Melody spoke up first, admitting to herself that the guy was too sexy. "So, what's up, Donavon?"

"I need a favor," Donavon told her. "I need you to braid up my youngin's hair for me."

"Alright," she replied. "He works for you now, baby?"

"Maybe soon," Donavon stated as he cut his eyes back over to Knight and saw the young man watching the television.

However, Donavon was certain the boy was fully aware of what was going on around him, and he was willing to bet that he was right.

TWO

KNIGHT SPENT THREE HOURS getting his hair hooked up in some zig-zag-style braids after having his hair washed. He then tried to pay Melody, only to have her turn him down. He then caught the smirk on Donavon's face after the attempt.

Knight left after hearing Donavon promise Melody that he would be back later that night. Knight then followed him back out to the Benz.

"What I owe you?" Knight inquired once both he and Donavon were both back inside the Benz.

"Owe me for what, youngin?" Donavon questioned him as he was starting up the G-Wagen. "You talking about the hair?"

"Yeah!"

"Youngin, that was on the house, and because I wanted to do it for you!" Donavon admitted with a little laugh. "Tell me something, youngin. How many jobs you got? I see you work all over the city."

"Right now just three!" Knight admitted. "I just got the third one today. Why you ask?"

"Your father really doesn't do shit for you, do he?" Donavon asked, ignoring Knight's question for the moment.

"Let's just say if I don't work, I really won't eat!" Knight told him, meaning every word that came out of his mouth.

Donavon slowly nodded his head while he drove and thought for a few moments. He then looked over at Victor and asked, "You smoke, youngin?"

"Weed only. Why?"

"Let's smoke and talk some more. I may have a job offer for you if you're interested," Donavon told him as he glanced back over to see the young man's facial expression, which was still one of calm and relaxation.

* * *

"Jesus Christ!" Karinne cried as she pushed toward the crowded house party after once again being approached by another one of the girls at the party wanting to know about her new supposedly boyfriend she had who defended her earlier in the day at the store against J. Prince and his boys.

She found her girls standing at the breakfast bar covered with juice bottles and soda. But there were also bottles of Hennessy and Alizé as well as bottles of Corona and Heineken.

"Girl, we was just talking about you!" Gina said as Karinne walked up in front of her and April. "Karinne, you and Victor is on everybody's lips tonight."

"That's not all!" April spoke up. "Girl, I just seen Jason and even Chris; and you know both of them heard about what happened and are not trying to talk to you now. They think you got some crazy boyfriend now, girl!"

"Tell me about it!" Karinne stated with a roll of her eyes. "Just walking over here about five girls stopped me wanting to know who my new boyfriend is."

Karinne looked over at April as she all of a sudden stood up laughing.

"What the hell is you laughing for? You find this shit funny, April?"

"I'm just saying, Karinne!" April answered while still laughing. "You may as well start talking to Victor. He actually is cute if he did something with all that hair, and you may just be working with something, bitch!"

Karinne rolled her eyes and sucked her teeth as she walked off, leaving April laughing and Gina smiling and calling out to her. But she ignored both of them as she continued walking through the crowd on her way to the front door.

* * *

"Listen up, youngin!" Donavon began, after parking his G-Wagen in front of a white and gray house in the Miromar Lakes area.

He then turned and faced the young hustler and said, "This place is real important. You're the only person who knows me that I'm showing this place to. You understand what I'm telling you, youngin?"

"I get you, old school!" Knight answered truthfully, understanding what Donavon was telling him.

Donavon nodded his head in approval as he held Knight's eyes. He then opened his door and climbed out.

"Come on, youngin!"

Donavon locked up the G-Wagen and then walked around the front end of the Benz to see Knight waiting. He then saw his Puerto Rican lady, Rosa, who he actually trusted due to her proving her loyalty to him. He then led Knight up to the front porch where she stood waiting for them.

"Hi, papi!" Rosa said as she kissed Donavon's lips and hugged his neck.

"Rosa, this is my youngin, Knight," Donavon introduced. "Knight, this is my wife, Rosa. We at the family's house, youngin."

"Hola, Rosa," Knight greeted her back in Spanish.

Donavon listened as both Rosa and Knight spoke to each other in rapid Spanish. He was impressed and smiled at the young man before he interrupted the two of them.

"Ummm, can we get inside the house? I've got something to discuss with the youngin."

"Oh, I'm sorry, papi!" Rosa apologized, smiling at Donavon before the three of them entered the house.

Once they were inside, Rosa locked the door behind her while Donavon led Knight to the far back of the three-bedroom, two-and-a-half-bath home. He stepped into the master bedroom and then told Knight to hold on as he walked into his and Rosa's walk-in closet.

He then opened the wall safe that was inside the closet. He removed two ounces of hard from the safe, and then closed the safe door when he was done. He left the closet only to find Knight standing in the exact spot where he left him.

"Come on, youngin. It's class time."

Once they returned to the front room and sat down, Donavon laid the two ounces of hard onto the glass coffee table. He nodded his thanks to Rosa after she brought him everything that he needed to cut up the hard that he was preparing to give to Knight.

"Alright, youngin. I'm about to teach you how to make some money, but you gotta pay attention to what I'm about to teach you."

"I'm listening," Knight stated while staring at the hard, which he thought looked a lot like butter.

"Alright, this right here is what coke looks like once it's cooked up."

"Don, come on," Knight interrupted. "No disrespect, old school, but I know what that is! Dudes back in Flint were pushing that shit around the block all the time."

"Just hear me out, youngin!" Donavon told Knight, cracking a smile at the young hustler. "This right here is the butter hard, and what I'm about to show you is how to cut and bag this shit up. Normally, an eight ball goes for $100, but I'ma expect $75 back, and you can keep $25 from each eight ball you sell. You following me so far, youngin?"

"I'm with you, old school!" Knight replied as he kept his eyes locked on the straight-razor that Donavon was using to cut up the hard along with baggies and the sandwich-sized zip-lock bag.

* * *

Karinne left the party early after dealing with the bullshit as long as she could. She dropped Gina off at home, and then she and April went back to her house. April was spending the weekend at Karinne's, and Gina was supposed to come by the next day and all the girls would hang out.

Karinne then parked her Lexus in the driveway beside her mother's Jeep Cherokee Sport, which was alongside her stepfather's Ford F-150.

"We should have picked up something to eat before we got here," April told Karinne after the two of them climbed from the car.

"My mom just went grocery shopping," Karinne told April as they walked from the driveway up to the front door. "We should be able to find something to put together."

Once they got inside the house, Karinne locked the door behind her and the two of them headed straight for the kitchen to find something to eat. They grabbed more stuff than they were going to eat and headed straight for Karinne's bedroom.

"So, Karinne, what are you going to do about Victor?" April asked out of the blue as she sighed and fell back onto Karinne's bed holding a big bag of chips.

"What?" Karinne replied, shooting April a look while changing her clothes. "What do I care about him for? He's not my man!"

"Everybody seems to think so!" April stated. "And as you can see, every girl at the party thinks he's cute and was asking about him."

"What does that have to do with me, April?" Karinne asked as she climbed onto the bed beside her best friend.

"Karinne, stop being stupid, girl!" April told her. "What guy you know would have done what he did if he wasn't interested at least a little bit?"

"He was just looking out for me, April."

"Because he liked what he saw. Think about it, Karinne!"

Karinne sighed as she laid back on the bed and stared at the ceiling. She actually lay there thinking about what April was telling her, only to be interrupted in her thoughts by loud laughing. She looked at April and then they both looked out the window next to the bed. Karinne climbed from the bed with April right behind her and walked over and looked outside.

"Karinne, ain't that your dad?" April asked. "And who is that he's talking to with them braids, girl? His ass is fine!"

Karinne stared at her father as he stood talking with the guy who April had just described to her. She then noticed exactly whose house her father was parked in front of. She looked back at the young man standing next to her father and instantly recognized who she was looking at.

"Oh my God. That's Victor!"

"You lying!" April cried in disbelief as she stared a little harder to catch a better look when he turned around and showed his face. "Oh shit! That *is* Victor!"

Karinne ducked out of the window after seeing both her father's and Victor's heads swing around to look in her and April's direction. Karinne then shot April a look.

"Why you yelling, girl?"

"It was an accident!" April said.

But then she and Karinne peeked back out of the window just in time to see both Victor and Donavon embrace each other before Donavon turned and walked back over to his Mercedes G-Wagen.

Karinne looked back at Victor after she watched her father drive off. She ended up locking eyes with him before he turned to walk back into his yard. He looked directly at her again before disappearing inside his house.

"Girl!" April sang as she stood up smiling at Karinne. "Now tell me that didn't look like his ass was interested? And he's even tight with your dad, too!"

Karinne listened to April as the two of them lay back down on the bed. She honestly thought about what April was saying and wondered what if.

THREE

Three months later . . .

KARINNE LOOKED OVER FROM Eric to her right after feeling April nudge her. Karinne released her boyfriend and saw both April and Gina pointing out toward the street. She looked in the direction her girls were motioning, only to see the red-and-chrome-edged Maserati Ghibli pull up in front of the school.

"Who is that, girl?" April asked Karinne as she, Gina, and Karinne watched Knight climb out from the passenger side of the sports car.

He was followed by an older red-skinned woman who climbed out from behind the wheel with a short skirt on and smile as Knight walked around the car and over to her.

"Damn!" Gina said as she watched the woman stick her tongue down Knight's throat in front of everyone.

"I guess we know who she is now, huh?" April asked as she looked back at Karinne and saw the look on her girl's face.

Karinne watched Knight and the woman carry on until he broke the kiss and his woman smiled at him. The woman then waved goodbye and climbed into her car. Karinne kept her eyes on Knight even after his woman drove off. Knight then met up with his new best friend, Duke, with whom he was always hanging out. His friend was two years older than Knight, but they looked the same age and were about the same height.

"I'll be right back!"

Karinne walked off and left her girls and her man, Eric, with his boys. She walked across the student parking lot and called out to Knight. She saw both Duke and Knight turn around and look back at her.

"What up, Karinne?" Duke said as she walked up.

Karinne ignored Duke and stopped in front of Knight.

"Victor, we need to talk!"

"About what now, Kay?" Knight asked, noticing that she had one of her attitudes on display. "What happened now, ma?"

"Excuse me, Duke!" Karinne told him, grabbing Knight's hand and pulling him off to the side and away from a laughing Duke.

She stopped and then turned and faced Knight.

"What the hell was that, Victor?"

"What was what?" he asked as he dug out his vibrating phone he felt inside his pocket.

"Victor, I'm talking to you!" Karinne said, growing more upset as she stood watching him reading from his phone.

"I hear you!" Knight replied as he slid his phone back into his pocket.

He then looked back at Karinne and then changed the subject.

"I'ma need you to do something for me. Drop me off somewhere at lunchtime."

Karinne sucked her teeth, rolled her eyes, and then asked, "Where at, boy?"

"I need to pick up something. You got me?"

"You can't get that girl to come?"

"Karinne, what's up?"

Karinne heard her name and looked back behind her to see Eric walking toward her.

"Eric, give me a few minutes, baby. I'm talking to Victor right now," she turned and said to her boyfriend.

"Dude's gone, Karinne!" Eric informed her, nodding in the direction that Knight was walking.

Karinne spun around only to see Knight was, in fact, walking off with Duke. She instantly got upset again. She hated how easily Victor acted as if he didn't care about anything—not even her.

* * *

Knight broke off from Karinne after her chump-ass boyfriend walked up to them. He then got Duke to drive him to pick up his new ride about which he had just received a text. When they returned, he then kicked it with Duke out in front of his first-period class.

"So, what's really up, fam?" Duke asked with a smile. "You and Karinne still playing them games, huh?"

"Naw, playboy!" Knight replied while slowly shaking his head. "Karinne knows what's up. She just decided she wanted to kick it with that clown Eric, so I kept it moving, son. Let ma do what she do!"

"So you already stepped to shorty about getting with her?" Duke asked, already knowing the answer.

"What's understood don't need to be explained, my dude," Knight said, just as two girls walked past and called out to him.

Duke chuckled as he shook his head and watched his boy. But then he got serious.

"Real talk, my nigga. So you thought about my offer yet?"

"You mean the whole coming to trap out in Murder Grove where you at?" Knight asked, just as a cute mocha-complexioned female walked right up on him and wrapped her arms around his neck.

"Knight, why you ain't call me last night?" the girl asked as she pressed her soft C-cup breasts against his chest. "I waited up for hours for you to call me. What happened?"

"Business came up, shorty!" Knight told her after he remembered the girl's face but not her name. "I tell you what though. Let me call you tonight!"

"Yo, Knight!" Duke called in a warning tone of voice, getting his boy's attention.

He then nodded back down the hallway.

Knight saw Karinne and Gina walking up the hallway in their

direction. Knight locked eyes with Karinne and watched her face ball up. He reached up and removed shorty's arms from around his neck and gently pushed her back.

"Excuse you!" Karinne stated once she and Gina stopped in front of Knight and Duke.

She turned toward the female who was all over Knight and said, "Don't you got somewhere you wanna be right now?"

Knight watched the girl walk off after sucking her teeth, before he shifted his gaze back to Karinne, who stood mean-mugging him.

"What now, Kay?"

"Keep playing, Victor!" Karinne warned him while rolling her eyes. "You need me to still drop you off somewhere at lunchtime?"

"Naw! My man Duke got me!" Knight informed her before looking over at Gina. "What's good, cutie?"

"Hey, Victor!" Gina replied, blushing as she smiled at him.

"I can't get no hug, Gina?" Knight asked, accepting her embrace once she stepped into his arms.

He then cut his eyes back over to Karinne and wasn't surprised to see the pissed-off look on her face.

"Anyways!" Karinne continued, once Gina released him. "Victor, I need some money."

"What's up with that broke-ass chump Eric?" Duke spoke up.

"Excuse me!" she said, shooting Duke much attitude. "I do believe I'm talking to Victor, Duke!"

"Yeah, that may be so, but that's my dude!" Duke stated in all realness. "You got a man, but you asking my nigga for cash. You may as well cut off that nigga Eric and fuck with my dude, since everybody already knows you feeling my nigga anyway."

Karinne sucked her teeth, rolled her eyes, and started to walk off. "Come on, Gina!"

"Karinne!" Knight called out and caught up with the two girls before they got too far.

He grabbed her hand and stopped her.

"Ma, how much you need?"

Duke watched his dude hand over the money that Karinne had asked for. In return, he received a simple thank you, before she and Gina walked off. Duke simply shook his head and smiled as Knight walked back over to him.

"Don't say shit!" Knight told his boy, only to cause the two of them to burst out laughing in unison.

* * *

Knight left the school once lunch hour rolled around and rode with Duke in his Chevy Malibu. He saw Karinne with her nigga Eric in the student parking lot next to his Expedition. Knight turned back on his cell phone only for the iPhone to give off an alert letting him know that he had a message. He started to check the message when the phone began to ring inside his hand.

"Don, what's good?" Knight answered after seeing his mentor

calling.

"Knight, this isn't Donavon, papi! This is Rosa!"

"What's up, Rosa? Where's Don at?"

"Knight, listen!" Rosa told him, before switching to Spanish.

She told Knight that she needed him to meet her at her place in an hour to discuss something important.

"*Uno hora*!" Knight replied in Spanish before hanging up with Rosa.

"Bruh, you speak Spanish?" Duke asked, looking over at Knight.

"Yeah!" Knight replied. "I just said one hour, but I speak three different languages."

"Damn!" Duke said in surprise. "I ain't even know that shit, fam!"

"There's a lot you don't know, playboy!" Knight responded, smirking as he cut his eyes over at his friend.

Knight and Duke pulled up to the motorcycle dealership and turned into the parking lot. After parking, Knight led the way inside and wasted no time in stopping a salesperson to ask for Paul Wilson, who was the salesman with whom he was working. After waiting less than five minutes, the red-headed salesman arrived. Knight shook his hand.

"Everything ready?" Knight inquired.

"Just waiting for your signature and the last amount for the payment, and we're all done, Mr. McKnight," the salesman explained while smiling at the young man.

As Knight dug out the rest of the money from his pocket, he noticed the salesman's eyes lock onto the money.

Knight handed him the rest of the cash and said, "Let's get this over with. I've got other business to handle!"

* * *

Knight and Duke stood in front of the dealership for twenty minutes talking about Duke's idea to relocate the trapping location from Knight's house. This was where he spent much of his time chilling out on the front porch of his father's house when he wasn't hustling at the car wash, washing cars, or pushing his work to new and regular customers.

Both Knight and Duke looked up to see the royal blue, black, and white Yamaha YZF-R1 SuperSport bike that was being brought around front.

"Here you go," Paul stated, after parking the motorcycle and shutting off the engine.

He then climbed off and smiled at the young man who was now the new owner. Knight accepted the helmet and thanked the salesman. He then looked over at Duke and saw the look on his boy's face.

"Bruh, you serious?" Duke asked, smiling as he looked over the bike. "You seriously went and bought a motorcycle, fam?"

"Pretty much!" Knight answered, looking at the G-Shock on his wrist. "Fam, I'll have to catch up with you later though. I gotta handle something real important right quick!"

After embracing his boy and then grabbing his Gucci backpack, he walked over to the Yamaha and climbed on. He slid on the helmet and then started up the bike's engine. He gave the bike a little gas and pulled off toward the exit of the parking lot. He hit the brakes, and after glancing around the streets, he gave the bike some gas and shot out into the street, picking up speed and flying down the road.

* * *

Knight made it across town to Rosa's house ten minutes later, slowing his bike and parking in front of the house. He climbed off the bike, pulled off his helmet, and then saw Rosa standing at the front door.

"What's up, Rosa?" he said as he walked up to the porch and hugged her. But he noticed the look on her face and asked, "Rosa, you alright?"

"We need to talk, papi!" she told him as she took his hand and led him into the house.

She locked the front door behind her, walked Knight over into the living room, and had him sit down beside her on the sofa.

"Rosa, what's going on?" he asked her, not liking the vibe he was getting. "Where's Donavon at anyway?"

"That's why I wanna talk to you now, Knight," Rosa explained as she held on to his hand. "As you know, Donavon left to go pick up the new shipment as was planned, but something went wrong. I received a call from my brother, who let me know that he was arrested."

"Whoa!" Knight replied, not believing what he was hearing. "You mean to tell me that Donavon's still over in Puerto Rico locked up?"

"He's waiting to be extradited back here!" Rosa continued before she changed the subject. "Knight, I'm going to speak with Donavon about what I'm about to discuss with you now. But first I need you to understand that you may have thought that Donavon was the one responsible for all the drugs that he had and was giving to you as well. But in truth, he was able to get what he was because of me. My brothers are the ones responsible for all of the cocaine that Donavon was receiving, and I was the key piece."

"You're telling me this because?"

"Because I've been watching you these last few months, and Donavon has taught you very well. You've caught on a lot easier and faster than much more powerful men in the drug game. Now as we speak and because we all need to continue to live, I am willing to place you into the position of power, if you're ready?"

Knight thought about everything he was hearing and what was being offered to him. He focused back on Rosa before his mind shifted to thoughts of Karinne and all the things he and Donovan talked about concerning her.

"What are you talking about, Rosa? I'm listening."

Rosa smiled at Knight's acceptance of her offer and then said, "This is what I will do, Knight. We will start you off with half a key for now and see how fast you can move that. You will bring me back $10,000 from the half; but understand that this deal is only what it is because you are Donavon's adopted son, or so he used to call you. Can you handle that, Knight?"

"When should I expect the product?" Knight asked her.

"My niece and nephew are on their way here now!" Rosa informed him. "You should expect it by tonight, but no later than first thing in the morning, Knight."

OUR

KARINNE HEARD HER NAME as soon as she and Eric walked out of the school building into the parking lot. She looked in the direction of where someone had called her, only to see Knight jogging toward her.

"Kay, let's go!" Knight said as soon as he caught up to her.

He grabbed her arm and began pulling her toward the parked cars, only for her to jerk away from him.

"Boy, what's wrong with you?" Karinne yelled at him. "Why the hell you pulling on me like that?"

"Let's just go, now!" he ordered while grabbing her arm again.

"Nigga, what the fuck is wrong with you?" Eric barked as he snatched Knight's hand away from Karinne's arm.

Just as Eric was about to say something else, Knight interrupted him by swinging and smashing his ass in the face with a right hook.

"Oh shit!" somebody yelled out as Eric hit the ground, only for Knight to begin stomping his face.

"Victor!" Karinne screamed, just as Duke showed up. "Duke, stop him. Get Victor!"

Duke dropped his backpack to go get Knight off of Eric. But instead he joined his best friend in stomping on Eric.

Karinne screamed for Knight and Duke to stop, just as

somebody yelled that school security was coming, which caught the boys' attention.

"Karinne, let's go now!" Knight yelled again, shocking her but also getting her to grab his hand and move her ass.

She glanced down at Eric, who was laid out and balled up in the middle of the parking lot in front of the entire school. She allowed Knight to drag her stumbling toward her car.

"Knight, slow down!"

"We need to go!" Knight told her, pushing Karinne toward her Lexus. "We going to your house. Hurry up!"

"Where are you going?" Karinne asked, after seeing Knight jog off.

"I'ma follow you," Knight yelled back as he jogged over to his bike.

Karinne was shocked to see Knight jump onto a new motorcycle, but she soon snapped out of her stare as she unlocked her car door. She tossed her bag over to the passenger seat and then climbed inside. A few minutes later she pulled out of the parking lot and saw that Knight was right behind her, with Duke driving his Malibu behind him.

* * *

"What the hell is going on, Victor?" Karinne yelled as soon as she climbed from the Lexus once she was parked in the driveway of her house.

"Here!" Knight said as he handed over his phone to Karinne.

"Who's that?" she asked, refusing to take the phone.

"It's Donavon!" Knight told her, releasing the phone once she took it.

Knight then turned and walked back out front where Duke was waiting. Karinne watched as he walked off, and then placed the phone to her ear.

"Hello!"

"Karinne! Karinne! It's your dad, baby girl. Can you hear me?"

"Daddy? I can barely hear you. Where are you?"

"Baby girl, listen! I want you to listen to what Knight tells you. He's going to explain everything to you until I can see you. I gotta go soon, so give the phone back to Knight. I love you, baby."

"I love you too, Daddy," Karinne told her father as she walked out front and handed the phone back to Knight. "Daddy wants you."

Karinne watched Knight as he stood listening to whatever her father was saying. She held Knight's eyes until he finally hung up the phone.

"What's going on, Victor? Where is my father at?"

"He's in Puerto Rico."

"Puerto Rico? For what?"

"He's locked up and waiting to get brought back here, Karinne! Donavon may be facing drug charges."

"What the hell are you talking about drug charges, nigga?" she asked, shoving Knight in the chest. "Don't fucking play with me, Victor! Tell me the fucking truth!"

Knight told Karinne everything he knew so far, hating to see her crying. He wrapped his arms around her and rubbed up and down her back.

"Don't worry, ma. I got you, I promise. You don't ever have to worry!"

"Let me go!" Karinne cried as she pulled away from Knight, rushing back into the front yard of her house and up to the front door.

Knight watched Karinne until she disappeared inside the house. He exhaled, blowing out a lot of stress-filled air as he looked back at Duke.

"You alright, fam?" Duke asked his best friend, seeing the stress and worry on his face.

"Naw, my nigga!" Knight answered truthfully. "Shit gonna be alright though."

"What's the plan, my nigga?" Duke asked, since he was down for whatever his boy was putting together.

Knight explained that he was willing to check out the spot in Murder Grove and also that he was giving Duke a job working with him. He was going to train and teach Duke about everything he needed to know to make money dealing cocaine. Knight broke off from Duke and agreed to hook up with him later on that night once he was ready to get to work.

* * *

Unsure when she fell asleep, Karinne woke up at the sound of her phone ringing and the smell of fish being fried. She sat up and picked up her phone from the bedside table and saw that it was April.

"Hello!"

"Damn, girl! About time you answered the phone!"

"I was sleeping, April. What's up?"

"Bitch! We heard about what happened today at school with Victor and Eric. Word is that Victor got jealous when he saw you kissing and hugging up with Eric, and he snapped and beat the shit out of him!"

"April, don't believe everything you hear, girl!"

"So what happened, Karinne?" Gina spoke up, since she was also on the line.

"Y'all on a three-way?" Karinne asked them.

"Of course!" both April and Gina answered together. "So what really happened, Karinne?" Gina asked.

Karinne gave her girls the short version of what had happened after school, but she left out the part about her father's situation. She continued talking with her friends until her other line beeped in.

"Hold on, y'all!"

Karinne checked her caller ID and saw that Knight was on the other line. She sucked her teeth and started to ignore the call, but went ahead and told her girls she would call them back and took his call.

"What do you want, Victor?"

"I see you're still pissed, so I'll make this short," he told her. "I'm just calling to make sure you're okay. You need anything? You hungry?"

"No, Victor! I'm fine!"

"Alright. If you need anything just call me, and I got you, ma!"

"When is my father calling again?" she suddenly asked.

"I won't hear from him again until he gets back to the States," Knight told her honestly. "He'll call me once he's back, and I'll call you."

"You make sure you do that!"

"That's on my word, ma."

"Uh-huh! Whatever, Victor!"

Karinne hung up the phone with Knight, unsure why she was even mad at him. She began to call him back, but her phone began to ring. It was Eric's older sister calling her.

* * *

Knight checked out the Murder Grove area that Duke had told him about. He met with a woman who lived there who smoked. Knight made a business deal with her about using her two-bedroom house to trap out of, and in return he'd pay her with hards that she could smoke. He also agreed to pay her $200. Knight and Duke checked out the house, which was practically empty, other than a sofa, couch, wooden coffee table, and 32-inch television. Other than those few items, there was very little else to which to pay attention.

Knight received a phone call from Rosa around midnight, letting him know that both her niece and nephew called from the airport. She explained that she was on her way to pick them up as they spoke.

"I'll be around your place by 5:00 a.m.," Knight told Rosa, before hanging up the phone with her.

Knight and Duke left the new trap house and passed a park that was just two blocks away from the house. He noticed that it was still somewhat packed even at midnight. Duke then dropped off Knight at his bike that was parked at his mom and step-father's house.

"I'ma get up with you tomorrow," Knight told Duke as they gave each other a pound.

Knight then started up his bike and made the trip back across town. He pulled up in front of his father's house and saw that his dad's girlfriend Rachell's car was parked in the driveway beside his father's Lincoln Continental.

Knight looked over toward Karinne's room window that faced his house and saw a faint light on inside her room. He made his way over to her window and then lightly knocked on the glass.

Knight saw the curtains move and Karinne's face appear. He stood staring at her as she stood staring back, until she rolled her eyes and unlocked the window. She then turned and walked away.

After climbing into her room, Knight lightly dropped to the

floor. He closed and locked the window, shut the curtains, and turned to see Karinne in bed watching television with very low volume. Knight then pulled off his shoes and his shirt and laid them on the dresser. He climbed into bed behind her. Both of them remained quiet for a moment and just lay next to each other until Karinne broke the silence.

"Tell me the truth, Victor. Do you work for my father selling drugs?"

"There's more to the story, Kay!"

Karinne rolled over to face Knight and met his eyes. She then admitted to herself that she had fallen in love with Victor a long time ago.

"Tell me everything, Victor. I wanna know the truth!"

Knight sighed as he wrapped his arm around her and ran his hand through her hair as she lay on his chest. Knight told her what she wanted, starting from the very beginning when her father first introduced him to cooked-up cocaine.

FIVE

KNIGHT LEFT KARINNE'S ROOM once she was asleep. He climbed back out through the window and stopped over at his father's house to shower and change clothes. He left his dad's house, got on his bike, and pulled up in front of Rosa's house ten minutes later.

He walked up to the front door and rang the doorbell. He waited a few minutes and was about to press the bell again when he heard the door being unlocked.

"Hey, Knight!" Rosa said half asleep, after opening the front door to see him standing there.

Knight followed her into the house after locking the door behind him. He walked into the living room, tossed his Gucci backpack onto the couch, sat down, and let out a sigh. He looked back over his left shoulder and heard talking, recognizing Rosa's voice talking on a cordless phone. He waited until she hung up the phone and dropped onto the sofa to his left.

"So, what's up?"

"That was one of my brothers I was just speaking with," Rosa explained. "He will be here shortly with the cocaine. He's also bringing my nephew with him because I want you to give him a job."

"Whoa!" Knight interrupted. "First, when was you going to tell me about your brother, and what do you mean give your nephew a job?"

"Relax, Knight!" she told him with a small smile. "My brother only wants to meet you. I've told you about my brothers as well as told my brothers about you. One of them has come to the States just to meet you."

"Alright! I can understand that, but what's this about giving your nephew a job?"

"That is a favor I'm asking you to do for me," Rosa explained. "My nephew got into a little trouble back in Puerto Rico, and my sister needed to get him away for awhile. I agreed to let him move here and live with me for a while, but he must work. I was hoping that a little of you would rub off on him and you could teach him a little of what Donavon has taught you. Can you do that for me, Knight?"

"What exactly is he good at?"

"Truthfully? He's known for using his gun back in Puerto Rico."

"So he's a gunman?" Knight asked, just as they heard the sound of a large truck or SUV pulling into the driveway.

"That must be my brother now!" Rosa stated, smiling as she stood up from the sofa and headed toward the front door.

She unlocked the door, stepped outside, and saw her brother and nephew climb out from an Escalade truck.

She smiled as they approached the front door. When her brother stepped onto the front porch, Rosa threw her arms around his neck and hugged him.

While Knight watched as Rosa hugged her sibling, he listened to their conversation they were having in Spanish. He sat waiting and continued to listen until Rosa first led an older Spanish man into the room, followed by a younger Spanish man who whose hair was in need of fresh braids.

"*Vea ese le*?" the brother asked Rosa in Spanish while nodding to Knight.

"*Si*!" Rosa replied, smiling as she switched to English. "You may as well speak English, Alex. He speaks Spanish as well, since he's half Puerto Rican and half black. Come and let me introduce you."

Knight stood up from his seat on the couch as Rosa walked over toward him with the two Spanish men. He stood face-to-face with the older man as Rosa first introduced as her brother, Alex.

"I've heard good things about you," Alex told Knight. "My sister says that you are a gifted young man for someone as young as yourself, and it helps that you're also the adopted son of my good friend Donavon."

"Knight, I want you to also meet my nephew, Stephen," Rosa introduced.

"*Qué pasa*?" Knight spoke up, nodding to the younger Spanish man.

"*Hola*!" Stephen replied, nodding his head in return.

Alex and Rosa watched as Knight and Stephen interacted with one another. Alex then looked over at Rosa and saw his sister nod her head in approval. He then nodded back as he handed Rosa the black leather duffel bag that he held.

"There's five keys inside. Are you sure about this, Rosa?"

"Have I ever been wrong about business?" she questioned her brother with a smile. "Just relax, and I'll handle things on this end."

"What about Stephen?" Alex asked as both he and Rosa looked over at Knight and their nephew.

"I've got plans for Stephen," Rosa told her brother while still staring at the young man. "He doesn't know it, but he's going to help protect our investment."

Alex looked over at his sister and saw the expression on her face, and quickly realized that she was putting together something inside her head. He smiled and shook his head in amazement.

* * *

After Alex left, Rosa sat down with Stephen and Knight and explained what her nephew's job description and responsibilities would be. She then turned her focus to Knight as she pulled out one of the keys of cocaine from inside the duffel bag and set it on the coffee table.

"Knight, this is what Donavon was receiving every week," Rosa informed him. "Five of these. But I'm going to start you off with half of this and see how fast you can move it. Once you're done, I'll have the other half ready for you as well. Do you remember what I asked for in return?"

"$10,000!" Knight answered, seeing a smile reappear on Rosa's lips. "Are you letting me get to work now or what? I'ma need the equipment to weigh this stuff and bag this shit up in, and I'ma cook it up while I'm already in the process."

* * *

Rosa left Knight and Stephen at the house, where Knight was weighing sandwich bags with dope to 29 grams, since the bag itself weighed 1 gram. Rosa then drove over to the apartment building where her niece and nephew were now living since moving from Puerto Rico. She pulled up in front of the high-rise apartment building's security gate.

Rosa drove through the guard gate since her name was on the visitors' list. She parked her car and then entered the building. She nodded in greeting at the doorman as she headed over to the elevators.

While riding the elevator up to the thirteenth floor, Rosa stepped off just as two middle-aged white men were getting on but paused to stare at Rosa. She ignored the two men as she approached the front door of her niece and nephew's apartment.

Rosa knocked and waited a few moments before she heard the door being unlocked. She watched as her sixteen-year-old niece swung open the door. She was as gorgeous as Rosa had remembered.

"Auntie Rosa!" Ayisha happily cried as she rushed over to hug her.

Rosa laughed as she returned her only niece's hug, and then they walked into the condo apartment.

"Come on, sweetheart. We need to get going, and I need to talk with you also."

"Mama said that you sent for me because you had something for me to do?" Ayisha asked as she and Rosa walked into the den.

"Your mother was right, sweetheart!" Rosa told her niece as the two of them sat down on the black leather sofa. "I have a job for you, but I'm sure you're going to enjoy it since it concerns you being friends with a guy I'm going to introduce you to."

"Will I get paid, Auntie Rosa?" Ayisha asked.

Rosa smiled at her niece and said, "Trust me, sweetheart! When you see Knight, that will be more than enough payment!"

* * *

Knight was still bagging up the twenty cooked eight balls he made from the two ounces that he had cooked up—ten from each ounce of hard. He set the sixteen ounces of powdered cocaine to the side. While he and Stephen were talking shop, the front door swung open and in walked Rosa.

"I see that you're just about done, Knight," Rosa said as she closed the door and locked it behind her.

Rosa walked into the room and stood beside the sofa where Knight was seated.

"What's with the powder? You're not cooking up the whole half?"

Knight shook his head in response, quickly finished what he was doing, and then looked up at Rosa.

"I'm pushing both hard and soft. I've noticed that different people want different shit, and I'm trying to be who they come to see."

Rosa smiled at Knight's response, loving his mindset. She then looked back toward her nephew.

"Stephen, your sister is outside in the car. I just took her to get registered at the same school as Knight. I now need to get you registered as well, but first you and I need to talk."

"Well, I'm about to leave!" Knight spoke up as he packed the rest of the dope into his backpack and then stood to his feet.

"Knight, just a minute!" Rosa told him, stopping him before he could rush off to work. "I have something you're going to need while you're out there working. Come with me."

Knight was really ready to go, but he respected her request, so he and Stephen followed behind her into a bedroom that was set up as an office. Knight stood and watched as Rosa walked over to a painting that hung on the wall, which covered a wall safe when she removed the art.

Knight waited until Rosa had opened the safe, and then he watched as she pulled out a gun, which he recognized as a .38 revolver. It was chrome with a black leather grip. He saw one once before in a gun magazine his father had.

"You know how to use this, Knight?" Rosa asked as she handed the .38 revolver over to him.

"Not a problem at all!" he replied truthfully as he checked the cylinder and saw each chamber was holding a round in it.

"Well, good then!" Rosa replied with another smile. "From now on I want you to keep that on you just in case, for protection."

"What I owe you?" he asked, sliding the .38 into the front of his jeans.

"Just stay safe!" Rosa told him. "That's payment enough."

After thanking Rosa and dapping up with Stephen, Knight headed back to the front of the house, with Rosa escorting him to the front door.

"What the?" Knight started as soon as he stepped out onto the front porch and saw a female sitting on his bike.

He looked over at Rosa.

"That's my niece, Knight. Her name is Ayisha."

"Ayisha, huh?" Knight repeated while staring at the vanilla-complexioned girl with the long raven-black hair that hung to the middle of her back.

He gave a small laugh but then remembered something and

looked back to Rosa, who was watching him.

"I saw something on the coke that I meant to ask you about."

"You mean the stamp, right? The picture of the cobra snake that's on the plastic bag of the cocaine?" Rosa surmised.

"What's the picture mean?" he asked her.

"Quick lesson!" she replied. "When you reach a level in the drug business, Knight, where you're supplying for a great deal of people, you need a stamp that represents who you are. That stamp you saw represents my family."

Knight nodded his head, enjoying the whole idea of having his own stamp. He then kissed Rosa on the cheek and started out toward his bike—and to meet the girl who was waiting for him on it.

Ayisha smiled as she stood watching Knight approach her. Rosa watched as the two of them talked, and she saw her niece flirtatiously touch Knight's braids. She shook her head as Ayisha wrapped her arms around Knight as he easily picked her up off his bike and gently set her down on her feet. Rosa also noticed that her niece still had her arms around Knight's neck while the two of them continued talking.

Once Knight climbed onto his motorcycle, slipped on his helmet, and then pulled off a few minutes later, Rosa stood waiting as her niece made her way up to the porch.

"Oh my God!" Ayisha cried as she walked up to her auntie with a big grin on her face. "Auntie Rosa, I think I'm in love! He is gorgeous!"

"I figured you would like him," Rosa said, just as the front door opened and Stephen stepped out onto the porch.

"Knight gone already, Auntie?" he asked, before he noticed both his aunt and sister smiling. "What happened? What's so funny?"

"Your sister thinks she has found her future husband," Rosa told Stephen with a big smile on her face.

"Let me guess, Knight?" Stephen asked, seeing both his sister and Rosa nodding their heads up and down.

SIX

KARINNE NOTICED THE CROWD as soon as she and her girls walked out of the school and into the parking lot. She spotted the motorcycle as the crowd shifted a little, after realizing Knight was at school after missing the whole day.

"Girl, ain't that Victor's ol' fine ass?" April asked, just catching a glimpse of him standing beside his blue, black, and white street bike.

"Yes, girl!" Karinne replied as she, April, and Gina walked up on the crowd.

"Yo, Karinne!"

Although she heard Knight call out to her as she walked past him and the crowd, Karinne kept walking, even though both Gina and April stopped. She made it to the driver's door of her Lexus just as Knight ran up to her.

"Kay, what's up?" Knight said as he gently grabbed her waist and stopped her from getting inside the car. "I know you heard me call you."

"What, Victor?"

"What up with you? What's with the attitude?"

"Where was you today? Why didn't you wake me up before you left this morning? You didn't even come to school today, Victor!"

"I was handling business!"

"Business, huh?"

"Kay, you know what's up, ma! Don't start tripping again."

"Whatever, Victor!" she told him, rolling her eyes as she attempted to get into the car again, only for Knight to stop her. "Boy, what do you want? Why the fuck you sweating me?"

Knight was a bit surprised but mostly caught off guard. He simply stepped back with his hands up after telling her to call him if she needed him. He walked off without saying another word.

Karinne watched him walk off, but she felt bad about yelling at him in front of everybody at school.

"Karinne, why you embarrass Victor like that in front of everyone?" April spoke up.

"Karinne, you was wrong for that, girl!" Gina told her. "You ain't have to do him like that at all!"

"Whose side y'all on?" Karinne asked, spitting the question at her girls, who quickly left the subject alone.

"Let's go get something to eat," April told her while watching the way Karinne was staring at Knight, who was now talking to his boy Duke.

"Come on, girls!" Karinne said as she rolled her eyes and climbed into her car ready to leave.

* * *

Knight watched as Karinne's Lexus drove off the school lot. He waved his hand dismissively at the Lexus and then looked over at Duke.

"Fam, what's up? You ready to get this money?" Knight asked as he was climbing onto his bike.

"Hell fuck yeah!" Duke answered as he took out his car keys.

"Alright! Follow me back to my pop's house so I can drop off my ride, and then I'ma roll with you," Knight told Duke, just before starting up his bike.

After leaving the school parking lot with Duke right behind him, Knight made the ride back to his father's house, just as his dad was getting home. He parked his bike out in front of the yard and saw his father blankly ignoring him, which was cool with him.

Knight walked over to Duke's car and told his boy to hold on a second as he jogged over to Karinne's house, where he saw her mother's car parked in the driveway. He rang the doorbell and then dug out his bankroll.

"Hey, Victor!" Barbara said, smiling after opening the door and seeing her daughter's extremely handsome friend from next door. "Baby, you looking for Karinne?"

"No ma'am!" he answered as he handed Barbara the money he had for Karinne. "Can you give that to Kay, please, Mrs. King? It's something for her to have to spend."

"Victor, what have I told you? I'm not married to Karinne's father, so you don't need to call me Mrs. King, and why couldn't you give my daughter this money yourself? Are you two fighting again, sweety?"

"I think so, ma'am," he admitted. "But can you give that to her for me, please?"

"Sure, Victor!" she told him.

She received a kiss on the cheek before the handsome and respectful young man walked off.

Once he was back at the car climbing into the passenger seat, Knight motioned for Duke to drive.

"Everything good, my nigga?" Duke asked as he was turning the Malibu around and driving back up the block.

"Yeah!" Knight replied, just as he saw Karinne's Lexus turning down the block. Knight caught Karinne's eyes for a moment as they drove by. "Let's just get this money, my nigga!"

* * *

Duke and Knight made it out to Murder Grove fifteen minutes later, passing the park that always seemed to be busy. Duke pulled up in front of their new trap spot and saw Emmy, the smoker and owner of the house, sitting outside on the porch smoking a cigarette. As Knight climbed out, Duke got out and called to her.

"What up, Emmy?"

"Hey, you!" Emmy called back as the two young boys walked up to the porch. "I take it you two are ready to work?"

"That's about right!" Knight stated as he handed Emmy the

money he promised her, with the rocks she wanted to smoke in between the bills.

Feeling the hard print of the dope that she was promised, Emmy said nothing more. She simply got up from her seat and walked off from the house to go enjoy herself.

After Emmy left, Knight and Duke went inside the house, where Knight broke down everything to him and showed his boy what they were working with. However, he was interrupted by his ringing phone.

He didn't recognize the number, but he knew the name, so Knight answered the phone call. "What up, Stephen?"

"What's up, Knight? This is my new cell phone, so lock me in. Where you at though?"

"Handling business. Everything good with you?"

"I'm trying to be where you at. Give me some directions, *hermano*!"

Knowing that *hermano* means "brother," Knight gave Stephen directions to the trap spot and then hung up after he repeated them back to him.

"Who that?" Duke asked as soon as Knight hung up.

"That's my—hold up!" Knight told Duke, hearing his phone ring again, only to see that it was Karinne. "Yeah, Kay!"

"Victor, where are you?"

"Taking care of something. Why?"

"What's this money for that you left with my mom?"

"Karinne, it's for you," he told her with a sigh. "You about to make an issue about me leaving you money, ain't you?"

"You know what, Victor! Don't even worry about it. I don't know why I even called your ass, boy!"

When Knight heard the line go silent, he looked at his screen and saw that Karinne had hung up on him. He simply sighed and shook his head in confusion about what he was doing wrong with her.

* * *

Knight was posted out on the front porch of the trap spot dealing with two customers who learned about him through Emmy. He allowed Duke to make the sale to let him get the feel of selling the dope they had to offer. He nodded his head in agreement when he heard Duke tell the two buyers to let others know about the new spot.

Within five minutes, three new customers walked up, and they were followed by two regulars Knight had called to let them know about the new trap location. While Knight took care of his people, he saw more buyers walking up to purchase the powder and hard. They helped all the customers until the last person was taken care of.

"Damn, fam!" Duke exclaimed as he stuffed more money into his pocket. "Whoever you getting that stuff from got some fine shit! You see how fast word spread? This spot's better than I thought!"

"It's the park!" Knight stated, just as he noticed a familiar looking Audi creeping in front of the house.

"Who that?" Duke asked as he stared at the car.

"I'm trying to figure that!"

"Knight! *Venir aquí, papaíto*!" the person called from the car.

"What the fuck!" Duke said after hearing but not understanding Spanish.

"Hold up!" Knight told Duke as he started walking out to the Audi and saw the driver's window slide down some more.

He instantly recognized Ayisha seated behind the driver's wheel of Rosa's Audi RS7.

"Hi, papi!" Ayisha called out with a smile as Knight bent down to look into the car.

"What's up?" Stephen said with a smile, seated across from his sister in the passenger seat.

"Why'd you bring her?" Knight asked him, nodding to Ayisha. "This ain't the spot to bring her around."

"Papi, it's my fault," Ayisha admitted. "I wouldn't let Stephen drive, so I drove him here. I'm sorry!"

Knight shook his head.

"Steph! Let's go, playboy!"

Knight then looked back at Ayisha and said, "Look! If you wanna talk to me, call me, Ayisha. You gotta phone, right?"

"Yes, papi!" she answered, pulling out her new iPhone. "What's the number?"

After giving her his cell number, Knight then told her to call him later. He stood back from the car window when Ayisha grabbed his hand.

"Papi, can I have a hug before you make me leave?"

"Yeah!" Knight answered, stepping back as Ayisha climbed her well-developed sixteen-year-old body out of the Audi.

She was dressed in a pair of jeans that hugged her high and phat-looking ass and thick thighs. He gave her a hug and, in return, received a kiss to the neck right before she lightly bit him.

"Can I see you after you finish working, papi?" Ayisha asked him as she started to climb back into the car, but peeked back only to catch Knight watching her butt.

"Call me, Ayisha," he told her as he pushed the door shut for her. "We'll talk then, shorty."

After Ayisha finally drove off waving goodbye to him, Knight walked back over to where Duke was standing with Stephen.

"Fam, just tell me one thing!" Duke began as soon as Knight stopped beside him. "Does your baby in the Audi got a sister that looks just like her? Shorty who just left is bad to death, bruh!"

"That's my man Stephen's sister, Duke!" Knight told his boy while nodding over toward Stephen.

"Oh shit!" Duke said. "My fault, homeboy. No disrespect, player!"

"It's cool!" Stephen replied with a smile. "I'm used to it, since everywhere my sister goes she gets the same attention. But it's Knight you may need to worry about, since my sister already said she was marrying him anyway."

"Damn!" Duke said, looking at Knight with a smile as his boy shook his head. "It's like that, fam?"

"There's money coming!" Knight said as he ignored Duke's question while nodding toward the two customers who walked up.

* * *

After two more new customers came through about thirty minutes earlier, a couple more regulars who Duke knew stopped by. Knight came up with an idea for the three of them to take a walk down to the park. But he then thought of a better idea and told Duke to hold down the spot until he and Stephen got back.

"I got it, fam!" Duke stated as he was dealing with two black dudes who stopped by for some powder.

Knight waited for Duke to be finished with the guys and then pulled his boy off to the side. He pulled out the .38 revolver that Rosa had given to him for protection, and handed the banger over to Duke.

"Use it if you have to. You get me?"

"I get you, fam!" Duke answered as he took the hammer and slid it into the front of his jeans.

"We'll be back!" Knight told Duke as he turned and walked off after nodding for Stephen to follow him.

* * *

"Yo, yo, Grip!" Terry yelled while grabbing his boy's arm.

Terry interrupted Grip as he was talking with some female, and then pulled Grip over beside him.

"Nigga, what the fuck!"

"Dawg! Check that shit out!" Terry told Grip.

Terry nodded toward the young light-skinned kid with the long braids who looked to be selling something. They also noticed that a nice-sized crowd was starting to grow around him.

"What the fuck is this kid doing?" Grip asked.

He stared hard when he saw three customers who bought powder from him go over and buy more from the kid. Grip started walking toward the kid, with Terry following behind him.

"This lil' nigga must be crazy or something!"

As they walked straight up to the crowd, Grip pushed through and almost knocked a guy over to get to the kid.

"Relax, playboy!" Knight spoke up when he saw the dark-skinned guys rush in. "Everybody can get served."

"Naw, naw!" Grip said, stepping closer to the kid. "Ain't none of that going on, lil' nigga! This shit here belongs to me, and you ain't selling shit out here!"

Grip watched as the kid who continued to make sales blankly ignored him. Grip then slapped the kid's hand down, just as he was handing a bag of powder to a dark-brown-skinned female. But he instantly froze up stiff as a black and chrome banger was swung out of nowhere and pointed directly in his face.

"What the—!" Terry started to defend his boy, but quickly shut up when another hammer was swung up and aimed directly into his face as well.

After Knight saw that both supposed hustlers were now bitched up and quiet, he gave a little laugh as he bent down to pick up the baggy that had been knocked out of his hand. He handed it over to the female buyer and winked at her. He then turned his attention back to the dark-skinned fake hustlers.

"What's your name, playboy?"

Grip was first going to ignore the young nigga's question; however, he quickly changed his mind upon hearing the click from the hammer in his face.

"Grip. It's Grip, and this is my dude Terry."

"Grip and Terry, huh?" Knight repeated. "Alright, Grip and Terry. We letting this shit be what it is for now!"

As Knight tapped Stephen on the back as they started to walk away, he was already putting together a plot inside his head.

* * *

After the two young niggas left after embarrassing him in front of the whole damn park, Grip angrily left the basketball court and walked over to the parking lot talking to himself. Terry followed behind him.

"Dawg, what's up?" Terry asked once he caught up with his buddy. "We getting at them young niggas or what?"

"Oh definitely!" Grip answered as he unlocked the doors to his BMW M5.

Once Grip got into his car and started it up, he pulled out his cell phone to make a quick call to his team. He then looked up at Terry just as the line was answered.

Grip barked out orders of what he wanted done and how he wanted things to be handled. He then hung up the phone and looked back at Terry.

"I wanna see how them lil' niggas handle this pressure I'm about to send their way!"

"You know where they at?" Terry asked.

"Yeah!" Grip replied. "I holla'd at one of them muthafuckers that bought a bag from that lil' nigga. He's telling muthafuckers where his spot's at, so I just sent our team out that way now!"

* * *

Knight and Stephen returned to the trap house and saw Duke handling business and selling work to a group of three buyers. Knight sat down on the porch steps as Stephen posted at his right and leaned against a pole.

"What's up, fellas?" Duke asked once he finished making the three sales.

He then walked over to where Knight and Stephen were standing, but he noticed the expression on Stephen's face.

"What's up with your man, fam?"

"We just had a lil' problem up at the park," Knight told Duke.

He then said something in Spanish to Stephen, who immediately walked into the house.

"Ya man looks like he's ready to fuck some shit up!" Duke stated, nodding behind Stephen. "What happened up there at the park anyway?"

"We ran into a little—" Knight began, but paused a brief moment when he noticed something. He caught on just as the car hit the gas and came flying up the block.

"Duke, get down!"

Knight leapt from the steps and knocked down Duke just as shots began ringing out. Knight covered his boy, Duke, with his body, but he peeked up to see Stephen run out into the middle of the street and let off rounds after the fleeing car.

Once the shooting stopped and the drive-by car was gone, Knight got up off of the ground and helped up Duke as Stephen walked back over, angrily speaking in Spanish.

"You're right!" Knight told Stephen in English, cutting off the boy. "We'll deal with them!"

"What the hell is he saying?" Duke asked, brushing himself off. "And what the hell just happened?"

"That was the outcome of the wrong decision I made back at the park just now," Knight explained. "But, like Stephen just said, I should have handled the problem right then, and this wouldn't have happened. But now I'll have to deal with this clown nigga Grip and his boy Terry."

* * *

Knight refused to close up shop, but continued to make what little business that came through. He also noticed that the Miami PD never even attempted to make a trip through the neighborhood after the drive-by. He called Karinne to let her know he was on his way over, only to get a surprise once she answered the phone.

"Hello!"

"Kay, it's Knight. I'm on my way to the house. Open the window, ma."

"I can't!"

"Why not?"

"Because I'm not home, Victor."

"Fuck you mean you're not home? It's almost three o'clock in the morning and you in the streets? Where the fuck you at? I'm coming to get you!"

"Boy, please! You doing you, and I'm doing me with my man. Bye!"

Upon hearing the line go dead, after catching the bullshit that Karinne had just told him, Knight took a deep breath to calm himself down.

"Fuck it! She made her decision!"

Knight decided to close down shop, and let Duke and Stephen know what the plan was. He then followed both guys over to Duke's Chevy Malibu.

"*Tu autorización*?" Stephen asked Knight from the back seat, just checking to see if he was okay.

"Yeah!" Knight answered in English. "Just thinking!"

Knight's phone began to ring right after dropping off Stephen at the condo tower that he shared with his sister.

"What's up, Ayisha?" Knight answered, after first looking down at his caller ID.

"Hey, papi! Why didn't you come up to say goodnight to me?"

"Ayisha, it's almost 4:30 a.m."

"Well then, you could have spent the night with me, or is it because your woman wouldn't like that?"

Knight smiled at peeping what Ayisha was trying to do. He then went ahead and fell right on into her setup.

"I don't have a woman, Ayisha!"

"Well, you do now, or aren't you interested in dating me?"

"What do you want, Ayisha?" he asked with a light chuckle.

"You as my man, papi! Can I have that, *papaíto*?"

"Yeah! You got it, Ayisha. You got that!" Knight laughed.

SEVEN

KARINNE ARRIVED AT SCHOOL the next morning with Eric after a planned night they were supposed to spend together did not go anywhere near as planned. Karinne spotted her girls Gina and April with a few other friends with whom they hung out. She picked up her bag once Eric parked his SUV, and then she climbed out. Eric called out to her, but she simply ignored him.

"Karinne!" April yelled as she and Gina started toward their girl.

"Ohhh!" Gina said after seeing Karinne's facial expression. "Karinne, what happened, girl?"

"Girl, what didn't happen?" Karinne replied with a roll of her eyes, just as Eric walked past her to meet up with his boys.

She shot his ass a look that told both Gina and April everything they needed to know.

"Karinne, it was that bad, girl!" April asked her best friend, with a worried look on her face.

"You two are not—" she stopped.

Karinne heard the sound of a motorcycle drawing close. She looked back behind her to first see Duke's Malibu turning the corner followed by Knight's bike. She continued watching both the car and motorcycle turn into the student parking lot and then pass by her and her girls.

"Karinne, who's that on the bike with Victor?" Gina asked while still staring at Knight as he parked.

Karinne heard Gina, but instead of answering her, she watched the female who was seated behind Knight climb off the back of the bike, pull off her helmet, and let down her long black hair. Karinne stared at the bitch who just climbed off the back of Knight's bike and was now hugging him.

"Girl!" April and Gina said in unison as they watched Knight with the Spanish girl.

But just as quickly, the two girls then noticed the Spanish boy who was climbing out of Duke's truck with braided hair that was just as long as Knight's.

"Who is that with Victor and Duke, Karinne?"

"I'm about to find out now!" Karinne told her girls, just as Knight and his friends walked up. "Victor!"

Victor walked by and ignored Karinne, so she called his name again. This time he stopped and looked back at her.

"What up, Karinne?" Knight said as he turned to face her.

Ayisha took his hand and stepped around beside him.

"Oh, so you don't see me no more, huh?" Karinne asked with an attitude. "Who's your friends?"

Knight heard Ayisha ask him something in Spanish, to which he quickly responded in Spanish back to her. He then looked back toward Karinne.

"This is Ayisha and her brother, Stephen. They're friends of mine."

"Looks a little more friendly than normal friends to me!" Karinne stated, eyeing up the female who was all under Knight. She rolled her eyes and then looked back at him. "Victor, we need to talk!"

"Now?"

"Yes! Right now!"

Karinne listened as Knight said something in Spanish to Ayisha and Stephen, and then he said something to Duke. She caught herself before she walked over to him and slapped the shit out of him, after seeing the Spanish girl plant a big kiss on his lips in front of everyone. Karinne then gave the Spanish bitch a look as the hoe walked passed her along with Duke and Stephen.

* * *

"Nigga, what the fuck's wrong with you?" Karinne went off as she rushed Knight and swung an open hand toward his face.

"Relax!" Knight told her, after catching her wrist in mid-air.

"Fuck you, Victor!" she yelled, snatching her hand away. "You just gonna disrespect me right in my face, nigga?"

"Disrespect you?" Knight asked with a light laugh. "Naw! Ain't no disrespect, ma! Like you told me last night or early this morning, I'm just doing me, so you do you! Ain't that what you told me while you was all up under that punk-ass clown you call your man?"

Karinne was unable to say anything, so she simply stared at Knight for a few moments.

"So that's your girlfriend now, Victor?"

"What you wanna holla at me about, Kay?" Knight asked,

changing the subject.

Karinne sucked her teeth and rolled her eyes, then asked, “What have you heard about my father, Victor?”

“From what I hear, he should be getting brought back here in two or three more days,” Knight informed her. “I’ve already set up our phones with collect calls. I went and had it done yesterday so Donavon can call you directly. You still got money left from when I gave it to Mrs. King?”

Karinne stared at Knight after he asked his question.

“So that’s who you wanna be with, huh, Victor?” Karinne heard herself ask Knight.

Knight sighed loudly and deeply, and then he ran his hand over his braids, which actually needed to be redone.

“Answer the question for me, Karinne!”

“What?”

“When I called you last night or this morning, and you told me you was with this clown you called your man, did you sleep with the nigga?”

“Victor, it wasn’t—”

“Answer the question, ma!” Knight cut her off before she could explain anything. “Just tell me the truth, Kay!”

“Victor, I regret it!” she told him, and immediately saw the disappointed look that appeared on his face.

Karinne tried to explain, only for Knight to kiss her on the cheek and then walk off, leaving her standing where she was, watching him leave.

* * *

Knight got through the first half of school and spent the lunch break putting in work and getting off the dope he was still holding while eating lunch with Ayisha. She then allowed him and her brother to leave and go handle their business, since the two kept talking about it and she had no interest in listening to it any longer.

Knight switched up his whole style of business and had Duke drive him and Stephen around all their old spots where he sold the dope for Donavon. He hooked up with his regulars and a few new customers to sell off the dope he was carrying.

Knight arrived back at school right as it was letting out for the day. He was waiting in the parking lot when Ayisha walked outside with another Spanish girl.

"Hey, papi!" she cried excitedly as she rushed over to Knight to kiss him on the lips. "Why's it look like you three are just now getting back to school?"

After chuckling lightly at her question, he nodded toward her friend and asked, "Who's shorty with you?"

"Papaíto, this is Jennifer!" Ayisha introduced.

But just when she was about to introduce Jennifer to Knight, Jennifer spoke up: "You don't have to introduce Knight. Everybody knows Victor Knight!"

Ayisha instantly noticed the way Jennifer was staring at Knight, and she found herself jealous. She cleared her throat, breaking the eye contact between Jennifer and Knight, and drew his attention back to her.

"Papi, I'm hungry."

Knight pulled out his bankroll and counted off $150 and handed it to Ayisha.

"That'll hold you off until later. Stephen brought you back the keys to the Audi, right?"

"You leaving, aren't you?" she asked him.

"Business, *mami*!" Knight told her.

He then looked up just in time to see Karinne watching him, but still standing next to her nigga Eric. Knight focused back on Ayisha and bent down and kissed her lips, only for their embrace to turn more serious once Ayisha wrapped her arms around his neck and deepened the kiss.

"I'm seeing you tonight, right?" Ayisha asked before she walked away, never allowing Knight to answer the question.

Knight chuckled as he stood watching Ayisha put on a show while walking away. He simply shook his head and started walking toward his bike, never noticing Karinne watching him from inside the SUV.

* * *

The young men arrived at the trap house after leaving school, but Knight first had a long talk with Stephen and Duke about bringing in at least two more workers. He thought it was a good idea since Stephen was really just his gunman and bodyguard. They agreed to the idea, and Knight allowed Duke to call up his cousins, Murphy and Sean.

Knight caught a few customers that came through the trap while they waited for Duke's cousins to arrive. Stephen tapped Knight on the shoulder just as he stepped away from him. When he looked over in Stephen's direction, he caught a glimpse of some movement in the bushes to his right by the sidewalk. Knight looked off just as Stephen took off in a sprint toward the movement.

"Hey!" Knight heard someone call out, looking over to the right again and seeing Stephen with a young boy in his arms. "Let me go! I wasn't doing nothing, man! Put me down!"

Stephen ignored the boy and carried him over to Knight.

"Look what I found!"

"Let me go, man! I wasn't doing nothing!" the little boy yelled while fighting to get away from Stephen's hold.

"Relax, youngin!" Knight told the boy. "What's your name?"

"Cam'ron. Why you wanna know?" the boy asked with much attitude.

"Alright, lil' Cam'ron, you wanna tell me why you was hiding out there?" Knight said, smirking at the boy's attitude.

"I was looking for somebody."

"Who?"

"Somebody named Knight."

"Why you looking for Knight?" he asked the boy, surprised to hear his name roll out of the boy's mouth.

"My momma told me to give him a message."

"Who's your momma?" Duke asked the boy.

"Who you, man?" the little man asked, looking Duke over and then back toward Knight. "You the one my momma said would be the one with the funny eyes. You Knight, ain't you?"

Knight smiled at the little man's awareness and his ability to pay attention to detail. Knight then nodded to Stephen to put the boy down, and then he motioned for Cam'ron to come sit down with him on the porch steps.

"Alright, youngin! I'm Knight. But why don't you tell me what your mom's name is, and this message she got for me that she would send you over here to tell me."

"My momma's name is Elayna Jones, and before she died, she told me to tell you that Grip's the one who killed her."

Knight recognized the name as the same woman who owned the house in which he was trapping. But hearing that the woman was dead and that the same person he was beefing with was the person responsible for her murder, Knight stared at the kid in surprise that he wasn't in tears.

"How old you, lil' man?"

"I'm seven!"

"Who you live with?"

"My mo . . ." Cam'ron started, but then stopped before he finished what he was about to say.

"It's cool, lil' man. I got you!" Knight told the boy, unsure what he was going to do or why he felt responsible for looking after the young kid. "Did your mom tell you where Grip was, youngin?"

Cam'ron shook his head no and then continued, "She just told me that Grip killed her and wanted me to tell you!"

Knight thought for a few moments about what was missing from the message. He then peeped the Ford Explorer that was slowly pulling up in front of the house. He sat and watched as Duke walked outside toward the SUV and then talked to the person at the driver's window. Knight then looked back at the kid just as a thought came to him.

"Lil' man, where was your mom when she died?"

"Brown Subs Apartment. We was at the park when Grip and this guy showed up and started yelling at my momma and asking who you was! They started beating her up when she wouldn't tell them!"

"Yo, fam!" Knight heard someone call out.

Knight looked over to see Duke walking over with two caramel-complexioned guys, one slim and tall, while the other was chubby but also had some height.

"Fam! These are my cousins I told you about," Duke told Knight with a smile as they walked up. "The slim one is Sean, and the fat boy is Murphy."

Knight nodded his head slowly as he looked the boys over. They both looked older than he did. Knight then stood up from where he was sitting and met both guys face-to-face.

"You two ready to put in some work?"

"Hell yeah!" Sean answered.

"No doubt, big homie!" Murphy answered Knight and nodded his head.

"That's just what I was hoping you two would say!" Knight replied, smiling a wide, devilish grin.

* * *

Knight made the trip out to Brown Subs Apartments after making a stop at Sports Authority and buying three wooden baseball bats. Knight sat inthe back seat of the Ford Explorer with Cam'ron right beside him. Murphy was at the driver's wheel, and Stephen sat in the front passenger seat.

Knight got directions from Cam'ron about where he last saw Grip with his mother. Murphy then drove around to the back side where the park was located. Just as Knight had thought, Grip and his boy Terry were seated on the park benches surrounded by a crowd.

"Y'all remember what the plan was?" Knight asked his crew, just as Duke opened the back door and both he and Sean jumped out of the SUV.

"Come on, youngin," Knight told Cam'ron as he climbed from the SUV and then waited until Cam'ron climbed out behind him.

With Stephen as an escort, Knight walked with Cam'ron at his side with his arm around the lil' man. He watched as Duke, Sean, and Murphy rushed right up into the crowd.

"Here you go, lil' man!" he told Cam'ron, just as Duke first swung his bat and caught Grip off guard and smashed him across the face.

Knight watched as Duke, Murphy, and Sean went to work, beating the shit out of Grip and Terry. They both screamed each time a bat slammed into a different part of their bodies. Knight looked at Cam'ron and saw the lil' man staring directly at what was going on.

"That's payment for what both of them did to your mom. Do you feel any better now, lil' man?"

Cam'ron slowly nodded his head, and then pulled away from Knight. He walked over to where Duke and his cousins were beating up Grip and Terry.

"Yo, Duke!" Knight yelled, getting his attention and nodding to Cam'ron.

"What's the boy doing?" Stephen asked while watching him.

Knight watched as Cam'ron took the bloody bat from Duke and began beating Grip with all his strength. Knight smiled a bit as he watched the youngin take out his anger for what had happened to his mother.

Knight soon heard the police nearby, and he knew that they were most likely heading their way. He then called out to Duke and waved Cam'ron back over so they could get out of Brown Subs before the Miami PD showed up.

EIGHT

KNIGHT GOT RID OF the rest of the work he had from the half key, finishing two days before the week had ended. He took Rosa the $10,000 he owed her and then picked up another half on which to get to work. He cooked up the dope for Duke and his cousins, who then put it out on the streets. He also took care of getting a new location for him and Duke to trap, and he let Sean and Murphy push what they were holding at the park since the police had the house they were using on lockdown.

Knight got a small one-bedroom apartment at Cloverleaf Apartments, which turned out to be a good spot out of which he and Duke could trap. Knight also had Melody get him a two-bedroom apartment at the Hollywood Oaks complex for him and Cam'ron. The boy had told Knight that he wanted to live with him instead of his aunt, who he did not really like.

Knight finished up with the second half a key faster than the first half Rosa had given him and once again took her the $10,000 she wanted for the half a key. In return, Knight finally got his hands on a whole key, which Rosa trusted in his hands.

"$20,000 back, right?" Knight asked Rosa, before leaving her house with the new brick of coke.

Rosa nodded her head and smiled as she watched the young man walk out of her front door. She kept her eyes locked on him, but she couldn't help wondering what her niece was doing and why she was not with Knight, since she knew that the young man now had his new apartment. She reminded herself to call and talk with her niece.

* * *

Knight dropped off more work for Sean and Murphy after leaving Rosa's house and then rode out to the apartment where he and Duke were now trapping. After he dropped off the dope and was just getting ready to leave, his cell phone went off.

Knight saw an unfamiliar name and number on his caller ID and almost ignored it. But he thought better and answered the call.

"Hello."

"This is a collect call from a correctional—"

"About fucking time!" Knight said out loud as the operator went through all the prompt recordings.

Knight locked up the apartment and was walking back out to the parking lot when he was given directions on how to answer the collect call. He then pressed "5" on the keypad and accepted the call.

"Knight?"

"What's up, old man?" Knight said, smiling at the sound of his mentor's voice. "You finally made it back, huh?"

"Late this morning," Donavon told him. "Where you at, youngin?"

"I was working."

"I'm not surprised. But listen, I need you to come out here to visit me. I need to talk face-to-face with you."

"You want me to bring Karinne with me, pops?"

"Yeah, bring her with you."

Knight continued talking with his mentor until Donavon let him go. He hung up the phone and then called Karinne.

"Hello!"

When Knight heard a male voice answer the phone, he balled up his face.

"Who the fuck is this?"

"This that nigga Knight isn't it?"

Knight quickly realized just who he was talking with and said, "Put Karinne on the phone, nigga!"

"She's busy as fuck, nigga. Her mouth's too busy sucking this dick, so try some other time, bitch!"

Knight heard the line die in his ear. He kept his calm and instead pulled up April's number and called.

"Hello!"

"April, this is Victor! I need a favor, cutie."

"What you need, Victor, boo?"

"Call Karinne on a three-way and see if you can get her on the phone for me."

"You two still fighting?"

"Naw! It's that nigga Eric. Dude really thinks I'm something to play with, and he got Karinne's phone right now!"

"Hold on, boo!"

Knight waited while April switched the line to call Karinne's phone. He heard the line ring when she switched back over connecting all three lines.

"Boo, you there?" April asked.

"Yeah, April."

"Who this?" Eric answered once again.

"Eric, what you doing answering Karinne's phone, boy?"

"She asleep," he admitted. "She went out with my sister and mom, and they just got back a little while ago."

"Wake her up for me. It's really important, Eric."

After a few minutes, April began to call out to Knight, just when Karinne's sleepy voice came over the line.

"Hello!"

"Karinne, this April, girl!"

"What's wrong, April? Eric says it's important."

"Girl, your husband, Victor, on the phone," April told her. "He needs to talk to you!"

"Kay!" Knight spoke up.

"What, Victor?" Karinne replied with a sigh into the phone.

Knight ignored her attitude and said, "Look, Karinne. Whatever you doing ain't my business; but when Donavon tells me to do something, I do it. So you need to meet me at your house in fifteen minutes, or I'ma just explain to your father that that punk-ass nigga you laid under is more important than seeing him. You decide!"

After hanging up the phone on both April and Karinne, Knight sent a quick text message to his lil' man, Cam'ron, and then he started up his bike and was flying away from the apartment building a few minutes later.

* * *

Karinne pulled up in front of her mother's house twenty minutes after hanging up with April, once Knight hung up on them both. She saw Knight's bike parked in her mother's yard, and then she noticed him sitting on the porch eating a sandwich.

After getting out of her car, she walked into the yard and stared straight at Knight as he calmly sat eating. She then stopped in front of him.

"How long you been here?"

"Too long!" Knight replied. "I told you fifteen minutes!"

"First off, you don't tell me!"

"Victor, honey, you want . . . Oh, Karinne, baby!" Mrs. King said, after seeing her daughter. "How long have you been here?"

"I just got here, Mom!" Karinne told her, just as Knight stood up and handed her mother back the glass cup out of which he had been drinking.

"Thanks, Mrs. King!" Knight told Karinne's mother, kissing her on the cheek. "I promise to come by and see you more often."

"You leaving, sweety?" Mrs. King asked him.

"Yes ma'am!" Knight replied. "I need to take Karinne somewhere, but I'll be back to see you."

Karinne watched as Knight walked out to her car and pulled out his phone. She then looked back at her mother.

"Karinne, sweetheart, I know you're at that age, but take my advice, sweety. That boy loves you whether he tells you or not. He goes out of his way to show you, but you're not paying attention to it, even though it's right in front of your face!"

"Mom, he has a girlfriend," Karinne told her.

"Yes, I know!" Mrs. King replied, but then added, "But whenever you call or you need him or something, where is he at? I tell you what. Test him, Karinne."

"Test him how?"

"Think of something. Now go on out there with that boy."

Karinne hugged her mother and then walked out to her Lexus. She caught Knight following her with his eyes. She unlocked the car doors, and then the both of them climbed inside.

"Where are we going exactly, Victor?" Karinne asked as she started up the car and pulled off.

"Donavon's at the main jail," Knight told her as he laid his head back onto the headrest and shut his eyes. "He wants to see us both."

"Why didn't you call me yourself? Why have April call on a three-way call?" she asked him, before adding, "Your little girlfriend wouldn't let you call me?"

Karinne looked over when she heard Knight chuckling. He had a smile on his face. She wanted to scream at him when he didn't respond. But Knight just sat back with his eyes shut as if he didn't hear her.

* * *

Knight and Karinne arrived at the downtown Miami Dade County Jail and went through the process of getting a visit with Donavon King. They both ended up waiting another two hours until a smiling and flirtatious female guard called out Knight's name.

They took the elevator up to the fourth floor with the flirting guard standing behind them. Karinne grew a bit jealous, but she controlled herself to keep from going off on the fat and nasty-looking guard.

"Check in with the guard at the window, handsome," the female guard told Knight with a smile and wave.

Knight and Karinne did as they were told and checked in with the guard behind the glass booth. They were then shown to the visitation window with a stool, which Knight then motioned for Karinne to sit on while he remained standing.

Knight remained quiet for a moment while they waited for their visitation. He stood with his head back against the wall and his arms folded across his chest. When Karinne called his name, he lifted his head up and looked at her.

"Yeah!"

"Are you happy?"

"Am I happy with what?"

"With that girl?" Karinne told him. "Are you happy with her?"

"Karinne, why you asking me this now?" Knight questioned her with a sigh. "You made your decision, and I'm seeing someone now!"

"But are you happy?" Karinne asked again as she stood up in front of him. "I remember you telling me once that I'm the—"

"Karinne, we not going there!" Knight cut her off, just as he saw Donavon enter the visitation booth. "Here's your pops!"

Karinne looked through the booth window just as her father walked up to the glass. She smiled at the sight of him, even though he had a full beard that had a lot of gray hairs in it. She picked up the phone at the same time her father did on his side.

"Hi, Daddy!"

"Hey, baby girl!" Donavon replied, smiling at his gorgeous daughter. "You're still as beautiful as ever! How you been doing?"

"I'm good!"

"Are you really, Daddy?"

"I will be, baby! I just need to get a few things in order, and things will be good!" he told his daughter.

Donavon then changed the subject to her and Knight.

"You and my youngin looked real close just now. Y'all finally stop all that child's play and got together yet?"

"Victor has a girlfriend, Daddy," Karinne replied, lowering her eyes.

"Oh does he?" Donavon asked as he shifted his gaze to Knight.

His eyes then met with those of the young man he considered his very own son.

"So are you seeing someone, Karinne?"

"Daddy, it's—"

"Baby girl, I know you!" Donavon stated, cutting his daughter off and focusing back onto her. "What did you do to push Knight into a relationship with somebody else?"

"Daddy, he has a lot of older women trying to talk to him."

"But until now has the boy ever seriously dated any of them, or has he spent a little time with them?" Donavon asked his daughter. "Karinne, I raised that boy and I know what he's like, because I taught and talked with him; and what you don't know is that that boy's feelings are a lot more serious than you may think. I tell you what. Try talking to him and ask him how he feels about you, and you'll be seriously surprised, Karinne. Now let me talk to my son for a few minutes."

Karinne stood up and passed the phone over to Knight, only for Knight to motion for her to sit down. She looked back at her father and saw him smile.

"What's up, Pops?" Knight said into the phone.

"What's up, youngin?" Donavon said with a small smile. "You look good. How's business going?"

"Business doing good, Pops," Knight answered. "Yeah! I also dropped $500 on your account and paid the $200 you owed. I also put some more minutes on both mine and Karinne's phones; and I even put some minutes on Mrs. King's phone so you can call her. Melody said to call her, too."

Donavon nodded his head seeing how on-point his youngin was.

"Here's what I need you to do, Son. First, I want you to go out to an address I'm about to give you. It's a Boca Raton address, and it's a house that has Karinne's mother's name on it. You'll find a toolshed in the backyard. Inside the back of the shed you need to dig up the ground. I've left money there which I've got plans for you to use when I hopefully get out of this place. I also need you to tell Melody to give you my contact numbers to all of the buyers I was doing business with, youngin. I'm about to introduce you to a part of the game that I've been training you for. You with me, Son?"

"Until my heart stops beating, Pops!" Knight answered, meaning every word that left his mouth and rolled off of his lips.

* * *

Once they left their visitation with Donavon and he was escorted back to his cell, Knight and Karinne left the jail and walked outside to her Lexus. They both had a lot on their minds after their talk with Donavon.

"Victor, can you drive, please?" Karinne asked him, handing him her keys.

"You alright, ma?" Knight asked, staring across at Karinne with a concerned expression on his face.

"Yeah, I'm just tired," she replied as she opened the car door and climbed into the passenger seat.

Knight glanced over at Karinne once he got behind the wheel and saw the look on her face. He reached over and gently brushed the hair back out of her face, which caused Karinne to turn her head and look over at him to meet his eyes.

"Ma, you sure you okay?"

"I'm just tired, Victor," she said with a nod of her head.

"Alright, Karinne! I'ma get you home now, ma," Knight promised her as he started up the Lexus.

Karinne sighed softly while she continued to watch Knight. She took in every curve of his handsome face; and before she even realized it, she had her hand gently stroking the side of his face.

"Victor, do you love me?"

Knight was surprised at the sudden question and looked from the road over into Karinne's eyes.

"Ma, where that come from?"

"My mom and dad keep telling me all of this stuff about you and how you feel about me, but you never tell me. Yet my parents feel that you're supposedly the guy I should be with. Do you love me? I wanna know!"

"What good would the answer to that question do, Kay?" Knight asked as he focused half on the road and half on Karinne. "You've decided that you wanted this clown Eric, and I'm with Ayisha."

"That can be fixed!" she told Knight, smiling a bit as she shut her eyes while he simply stared back at her.

Knight made it back to Karinne's mother's house and pulled the Lexus up in front of her yard. He saw the SUV that was all too familiar parked in front. He peeped both Eric and Mrs. King's husband who were posted out on the porch talking. He then parked the Lexus and woke up Karinne.

"Ma, wake up!" Knight said gently, shaking her awake. "Ma, we're here!"

Karinne sat her seat back upright, not even remembering that she laid it back. With a sleepy smile, she looked over at Knight, but was startled by a knock on her window. She quickly spun around to see that it was Eric.

"Eric, what are you doing here?" Karinne asked as she climbed out of her Lexus.

"You wasn't answering your phone," he answered as he shot Knight a hateful look before focusing back on Karinne. "What the fuck is you doing with this nigga, Karinne?"

"Eric, don't start! Please!" Karinne begged as she slammed the car door.

Eric grabbed Karinne's arm as she started to walk away, and then jerked her back and pushed her against the car.

"Answer my fucking quest—!"

Eric was unable to finish what he was in the middle of saying as pain exploded in the right side of his face. He stumbled to his side and dropped to his knees in a daze.

"Victor, please!" Karinne begged after seeing him swing at Eric.

She looked down as Knight handed her something.

"Oh God!" Karinne yelled when she saw that it was a gun.

"Hold that a second," Knight told her as he pulled off his shirt and wifebeater.

He then stepped over to Eric and said, "Get up, nigga! You been asking for this shit, so I'ma give it to you."

"Karinne, what's going on?" Marsha asked as she rushed out to her daughter.

She saw both Knight and her daughter's boyfriend, Eric, about to fight in the middle of the street.

Karinne heard her mother but watched as Eric rushed Knight in the middle of the street. Knight immediately side-stepped and swung a right that smashed into the side of Eric's face, which made him stagger back a bit. Karinne stood and stared as she watched Knight continue to beat on Eric, who fought wildly while trying to land a blow.

"Victor!" she yelled, seeing her mother's husband rushing up behind Knight

Karinne next saw Knight spin around and duck, but return a right hook that smashed into Mrs. King's husband's stomach, which dropped him to his knees.

Knight looked down at Mrs. King's husband and then over at Eric, who was on his ass with blood pouring from his nose and mouth. Knight shook his head at the sight and then walked off and headed back over to Karinne.

"Victor!" Karinne cried.

But she couldn't find anything else to say. So Knight picked up his shirt and then walked over to her. He then grabbed the gun that she forgot she was holding for him.

"That's who you choose, huh?" Knight asked Karinne.

He then kissed Mrs. King on the cheek before walking over to his bike, leaving both mother and daughter watching him drive away.

Karinne was still watching Knight even as he drove off down the street. She then looked at her mother.

"This boy's fighting about you now, Karinne. You need to fix this and soon, girl!" her mother explained.

NINE

KNIGHT STOPPED AT MELODY'S apartment after leaving Karinne's house. He parked his bike and then walked into her building, just as his phone rang from inside his pocket. He dug out his iPhone and saw that it was Stephen calling, right when he got to Melody's front door.

"Where you at, *hermano*?"

"Picking up Cam'ron," Knight informed him as he kissed Melody's cheek as he entered the apartment.

"I'm with Duke now, but we pulling up at the spot now. You coming through?"

"I gotta handle something first," Knight told him as he sat down on the sofa where Cam'ron sat playing Xbox One. He held out his fist to the youngin and received a pound in return. "Let Duke know that's already there, and I'll be through later."

"You holding?"

Knight smiled at the normal question Stephen asked him.

"I'm good, my hermano!"

Knight hung up his phone and then looked over at Cam'ron and asked, "What's up, lil' man?"

"Hey!" Cam'ron replied as he continued playing Call of Duty.

"You took care of your homework, right?"

"Yeah!"

"My man!" Knight stated with a big smile as he proudly rubbed the back of his little man's head.

He then looked over and saw Melody standing in the entrance of the hallway watching him. A smile was also on her face.

Knight stood up from the sofa and walked over to Melody as she turned and led him back into the bedroom. Knight then looked around and noticed that she had changed up a few things the master bedroom.

"You remind me so much of when Donavon first brought you over here every time I see you with Cam'ron, Knight," Melody told him with a grin. "Donavon trained you to be a good man, Knight."

"He wants you to come up to the jail to see him this weekend," he told Melody. "Donavon's back in the States now."

"Why didn't he call me?"

"He's calling tonight!" Knight replied. "I'ma need another favor though."

"What is it, Knight?" she asked as she saw Donavon for the first time in the handsome boy who stood in front of her.

"I'ma need to hold your car for a little while!" he told her. "I gotta handle something for Donavon, and I can't be carrying this shit 'round on my bike, since I don't know what all I'ma find when I get to where I'm going."

"Why don't you just buy a car, Knight? I'm sure you got the

money for one!"

"Right now I don't have the time to look, what with school in the morning and hustling at night. I don't really have the time!"

"You like SUVs?" she asked him. "This guy I know who stays in this same complex has a 2015 GMC Denali for sale."

"What he want for it?"

"Because it's already fixed up, he's asking $40,000 for it as is."

"Is it worth it, Melody?"

"For you, yes!"

"Alright!" Knight said with a nod of the head. "On your word, tell him to bring it around here! I want it now!"

"Alright, young Donavon," Melody said jokingly while smiling as she walked over to her dresser to pick up her cell phone.

She paused when she heard Knight call her name.

"Yeah, Knight!"

"I also gotta get Donavon's contact book he said that you're holding for him," Knight explained, to which he received a nod and a smile.

* * *

Ayisha heard a knock at her front door just as she was walking out of the kitchen and talking on the phone. She turned toward the front door and looked out the peephole to see her Auntie Rosa. She unlocked the door and opened it.

"Hey, Auntie!" Ayisha said as Rosa entered her apartment and then locked the door behind her.

"What are you doing here, Ayisha?" Rosa asked, turning to face her niece. "Why aren't you with Knight?"

"He left school early, Auntie," Ayisha explained as the two of them walked into the den. "How can I get close to him if I can't keep up with him? He barely stops at the condo with me and Stephen, and I just found out that he has a new apartment with the little boy he supposedly took in and is taking care of."

"Well, if you can't keep up with him, why is it you aren't making him keep up with you?" Rosa asked her. "What's the whole reason I sent for you, Ayisha? If you can't do this simple thing I've asked, I'll just send you back to Puerto Rico and I'll find someone that will be able to do this simple job for me. Are we understood?"

"Yes, Auntie!"

"Good!" Rosa stated. "Call your brother and find out where Knight is, and you find your way to where he is and do whatever you must to get his full attention. Because I refuse to lose this young boy! He is worth a lot of money as long as he is doing business with this family, and you are going to be the hold that keeps him tied to this family!"

* * *

"Oh my God, Karinne!" April cried as she and Gina sat inside her bedroom listening to the story about the fight between Knight and Eric.

"Karinne, are you serious?" Gina asked, unable to believe the story about how the always calm and cool Victor Knight had just snapped. "Victor really went off on Eric like that?"

"Eric's ass is back in the hospital with a broken jaw!" Karinne told her girls while actually smiling. "But you're not gonna believe this though. Eric's ass got the nerve to break up with me and say it's my fault he's in the hospital."

"He ain't lying!" April said, causing both Gina and Karinne to shoot her looks.

"Everybody knows how crazy Victor is about Karinne, but Karinne's the only one acting like she can't see that boy in love with her; and now she sitting here acting like she don't know what the hell is going on. I don't like Eric's ass myself, and everybody knows that Victor's your boo but Eric, right Karinne? You knew this shit was going to happen. My question now is, what you gonna do?"

"What do you mean, what am I going to do?" Karinne questioned. "What am I supposed to do?"

"Karinne, you can't be that slow, bitch!" April said, shaking her head sadly. "You just gonna let that fake-ass, Spanish Jennifer Lopez take your man, or are you going to go get your man back?"

"Hold on!" Karinne told her girls after a moment's thought.

She picked up her cell phone and pulled up Knight's number.

"Yeah, Kay?" Knight answered in the middle of the second ring.

"Victor, where are you?"

"What's up, Kay? I'm handling something right now."

"I wanna see you. We need to talk about . . . us!"

Knight remained quiet a few moments and then asked, "Where you at? You with April and Gina?"

"I'm at home, Victor," she told him, smiling as she looked over at her girls.

"Alright! Gimme about an hour and I'ma come by and pick you up. Now can I get back to what I was doing, please!"

"Bye, boy!" Karinne answered, smiling as she hung up the phone.

Karinne shook her head and was still smiling, and then answered, "He knew I was with you two, but he's coming over to supposedly pick me up in an hour."

"So why you smiling?" Gina asked, with a grin on her face as well.

"Girl, I don't even really know!" Karinne stated as she climbed off of her bed and walked over to her closet.

"What you about to do now?" April asked.

"Girl, I need to get ready for my new man to get here!" Karinne told her girls, laughing after hearing her own words when speaking about Victor McKnight.

* * *

Knight made it back to his and Cam'ron's apartment close to 6:30 p.m., after making the trip out to the house in Boca Raton that

Donavon had told him about. The house had a team of live-in servants that maintained the five-bedroom, six-bath, two-story house. Knight showered and changed into a Gucci outfit along with a pair of Gucci loafers. He then took what was needed for the lawyer for Donavon from the $100,000 that his mentor had buried at the house, and put the rest away.

Knight left the apartment once he was finished and climbed back into the 2015 GMC Denali that he had just bought. It was midnight sapphire in color with a jubilee-silver top and was sitting on 30-inch Asantis that were the same color as the SUV. He sent a quick text message to Melody asking if everything was okay, and then he sent a text message to Karinne letting her know he was on his way.

Knight's phone rang as soon as he sent the text to Karinne, only to see that Ayisha was now calling. He turned down Notorious B.I.G. and Mob Deep's "Beef" that was playing from the six 12-inch Thunder Square subwoofers that were inside fiberglass case with a Thunder Elite 1004 TE1501D amplifier.

"What's up, Ayisha?"

"Papi! Where are you? I've been calling you all day! I miss you!"

"I told you earlier that I had things to handle, Ayisha! What's up though?"

"When are you coming home, Knight? I want you next to me tonight."

"Ayisha, let me deal with—"

"We need to talk, Knight!" Ayisha cut him off. "Go ahead and handle your business out there, but then come home and handle your business here!"

After hearing the line die in his ear and listening to what Ayisha had to say, Knight looked at his phone screen and shook his head. He tossed the iPhone onto the center console and cranked the music back up.

* * *

"Hello!" Karinne said as she answered her phone after hearing it ring as she was walking into her bedroom from the bathroom.

"I'm outside, ma!"

"Here I come now!" Karinne responded, smiling just from the sound of his voice.

She hung up the phone and then rushed around, grabbing her Dolce & Gabbana bag and keys. She then ran from her bedroom and out to the front of the house.

"Bye, Momma! I'll be back later!" Karinne yelled from the front door.

"Tell Victor I said to call me tomorrow!" Karinne heard her mother yell back as she was stepping out onto the porch with a smile on her face.

She wondered how her mother knew she was leaving with Knight.

Karinne turned her head out to meet Knight at her Lexus, after locking the front door. But she paused in mid-step when she saw the big SUV parked in front of her house.

"What in the world!"

"You coming or not?" she heard from inside the SUV, recognizing Knight's voice once the dark-tinted window went down a little.

Karinne walked up to the Denali and over to the passenger door. She could hear the rumble from the bass. She opened the truck, which turned on the light inside. She saw Knight seated behind the wheel smiling a sexy-as-hell smile at her. She climbed up into the dark bourbon leather seat and closed the door behind her.

"What's up, ma?" Knight said, running his eyes over her in the tight body-hugging outfit she was wearing. "You looking and smelling good over there. Any reason?"

"Maybe!" she replied with a smile.

She then looked around the inside of the SUV.

"When did you get his truck, Victor?"

"Today!" he replied as he pulled off. "I need to drop off this money to your father's attorney. You said you wanted to talk though, right?"

"Yes, I do!" Karinne stated as she began to look through the MP3 player that was connected to the stereo.

She stopped at the song she wanted to hear and began to smile when Bruno Mars's "Just the Way You Are" played through the speakers. She began to sing the song to Knight. Karinne then took Knight's right hand from the wheel and intertwined their fingers as she continued singing.

Knight caught what Karinne was telling him through the song, and he allowed her to finish while he drove. He made it out to Miami Beach to the attorney's office, but once the song came to an end, he turned the volume down and got straight to the point.

"So you having a change of heart about us, huh?"

"I have!" she admitted, before asking with a bit of fear, "Am I too late?"

"Are you too late, huh?" Knight repeated the question.

But he released her hand again and picked up the MP3 player.

"What are you doing, Victor?" Karinne asked, just as her song "Catch a Grenade" by Bruno Mars came on, and Knight surprised her by singing the song to her.

She stared at him with wide eyes and with her mouth hanging wide open in total shock and surprise. She could not believe how good Knight sounded, and she was unaware that he could sing the way he was for her right at that moment.

As soon as the song came to an end and Knight had finished singing, Karinne was on Knight. They locked lips as the two passionately kissed until Knight broke the embrace to focus on the road after someone blew their horn behind him.

"Whoa!" Knight said with a little laugh as he glanced over at Karinne. "So I guess you understood what my message meant then, huh?"

"You just make sure you deal with that other problem with that long, black-hair gal who's been all over you lately, because I'm not going to share my man!" Karinne informed him with a big smile.

She took Knight's hand again and watched a smile fill his extremely handsome face. She loved when he smiled.

* * *

Knight met up with the attorney and gave him the $35,000 as Donavon had requested. He then gave him the message that Donavon wanted delivered. After they were done they left the officer, and the two of them planned to just chill together, until Knight's phone blew up with calls from Stephen.

"Steph, what's—?" Knight began, only to be cut off by Stephen, who was yelling about Duke getting hit and being in the hospital.

"What hospital?" Knight asked, now all about his business.

He sat up in his seat as Stephen told him the name of the hospital where he, Sean, and Murphy were waiting.

"Victor, what happened?" Karinne asked as soon as he hung up the phone.

"Duke's been shot!" Knight told her. "I'm taking you home."

"No the hell you're not!" Karinne yelled. "I'm going to the hospital with you! Duke's my friend, too!"

Knight wasn't in the mood to argue with Karinne, but he wanted to find out who was behind what had happened to his best friend. He hit the gas, which caused the Denali to pick up speed as they flew toward Parkway Hospital.

* * *

Stephen was completely pissed off as he paced back and forth outside the hospital in front of the entrance after hanging up the phone with Knight. He explained to his boy what had happened with Duke. Stephen then felt his phone vibrate, and he looked at the screen to see that his auntie was calling again. He sent her to voicemail, since he was not in the right mind to deal with her and her bullshit.

Stephen looked up when he heard the screech of tires and saw an SUV swinging into the parking lot. The GMC Denali slammed its breaks directly in front of him. Stephen already had a grip on his hammer, until he saw Knight jump out of the truck.

"Where he at?" Knight asked as he walked past Stephen and headed toward the hospital entrance.

Stephen called out the floor on which Duke and his family were staying. Stephen then noticed the familiar girl that Knight always fought with running from the SUV following right behind him into the hospital. Stephen got into the Denali and parked it, and then rushed back into the hospital to rejoin the others.

Stephen took the elevator back up to the third floor, where he could see Knight and the girl standing outside the waiting room along with Sean, Murphy, April, and Gina, all whom he had met before. He quickly jogged up the hall to join the crew and could hear the anger in Knight's voice, which was so out of character since Knight was almost always calm and soft-spoken.

"How is he?" Knight asked through tight lips.

"The doctor says he was shot in the arm and leg, but we don't know how bad!" April told Knight in tears.

"Who the fuck did this?" Knight asked, looking first over toward Sean and Murphy and then over at Stephen, with none of them saying anything.

"So don't nobody know what happened to my fucking brother, huh? Somebody needs to tell me something before I start—!"

"Baby, calm down!" Karinne said as she grabbed Knight's arm and pulled him away from the others.

Stephen watched his friend walk off with the girl who he remembered by face from school. He could see the anger and hurt on his boy's face.

Stephen then looked back at Murphy and said, "Give me the key to your truck."

"For what?"

"Just give it to me!" Stephen interrupted, speaking in English at first before switching to Spanish.

He then waved his hand for Murphy's truck keys.

After handing over his truck keys to Stephen, Murphy watched the crazed young Spaniard walk off in a huff.

"What the fuck he about to do?" Murphy asked his brother, Sean.

Sean shrugged his shoulders and then looked back down the hall, just in time to see Duke's mother heading their way.

"Ms. Williams!" April spoke up first. "How is he?"

"He's going to be okay, thank God!" Ms. Williams told April, just as Karinne and Knight walked up.

She spotted Knight and instantly reached out for his embrace.

"I'm sorry I wasn't there!" Knight told Ms. Williams as he held her tightly in a hug.

"Hush that up, baby!" Ms. Williams told Knight. "I'm just happy the both of you are okay, Victor. Duke is going to be just fine! He's going to need to wear a brace for his arm for a while, and the bullet that hit his leg was only a graze. But he's going to be just fine!"

"Can we see him?" April asked hopefully.

"Sure, sweetheart!" Ms. Williams answered as she led his friends back to her son's hospital room.

Once they were at his room door, Ms. Williams escorted them inside. April broke away from the group and rushed over to Duke's bedside and hugged him. She then began complaining about how scared she was.

"Baby, calm down!" Duke said.

He used his good right arm and grabbed April's hand, pulling her down to sit on the bed beside him.

"How you feeling, fam?" Knight asked as he walked up beside Duke's bedside.

"I'm good, fam!" Duke replied as he used his good hand to shake up with Knight.

"You know I'm sorry I wasn't there for you, fam!" Knight told him.

"I'm glad you wasn't, bruh! Ain't no need for both of us to be laid up in this place, you feel me?" Duke told him.

Knight nodded his head in understanding and then stepped to the side as Karinne stepped up beside Duke.

"Hey, boy! I'm happy to see you're doing okay."

"Yeah, I'm good, shorty!" Duke said, smiling up at Karinne before looking around the room. "What's up with the boy Stephen? Where he at?"

"He jetted off somewhere!" Murphy explained.

"Where?" Knight asked, looking hard at Murphy.

"I don't know!" Murphy replied, and seeing the expression he received from Knight, he continued, "The boy just asked for my keys and gave me these before he left."

Knight saw that Murphy was holding up his keys, which he took back and put in his pocket.

Knight then looked back at Duke and mouthed, "Who shot you?"

"I don't even know!" Duke answered out loud, before looking over at his mother. "Mom, can you get me some water, please?"

"Sure, baby!" Ms. Williams told her only son as she took the water pitcher April was holding.

Once Ms. Williams left the room and the door closed behind her, Knight looked back over at Duke.

"You see who it was that hit you?'

"It's crazy! Because one moment I was selling to this dude, and then the next homeboy was pulling out on me!" Duke told Knight. "Me and dude fought a few minutes until Stephen showed up and started showing out with them hammers he be holding. I think he hit the nigga, but by then, I was already hit and down!"

Knight simply nodded his head after listening to the scenario that Duke had just finished telling him.

"I'ma deal with this, fam! Trust me!" Knight promised.

Karinne heard the hospital room door open back up and saw Ms. Williams enter the room. She interrupted the conversation Duke and Knight were having. "Duke! When were you and April planning on telling us you two were dating?"

"That's just it, girl!" April said with a grin. "Everybody knew, but with you messing with sorry-ass . . . I mean, Eric . . . sorry, but you was left out of the news!"

"Oh, okay!" Karinne said, nodding her head with a sneaky smile showing.

"Ma, what you plotting?" Knight asked as he wrapped his arm around her waist and pulled her up against him.

He then wrapped his other arm around her and kissed her on her neck.

"Nothing, baby!" she replied as she lay back against her man's chest.

"Umm, excuse me!" April said, staring at the two of them. "Is there something you two not telling us?"

"Nope!" Karinne said, sticking her tongue out at April, which caused the others to burst out laughing.

TEN

THREE DAYS AFTER THE shooting incident when Duke got hit twice, the team was back to business, minus Stephen, who was still missing since he left the hospital the night Duke was shot. Knight met with Rosa and got guns for his entire team, since niggas on the streets wanted to test the team's gangsta, since they were all so young. He even got himself a brand-new Glock 9 mm, since he wanted something more than a piece that held only six rounds.

Knight had gotten rid of the brick Rosa had given him, so he paid her another visit, but with a different plan in mind.

"Hello, Knight," Rosa said, smiling after opening the front door to see Knight standing there looking handsome in his Gucci outfit.

Rosa noticed that he had obviously taken a liking to Gucci, since every time she saw him, he was dressed in it.

"What's up, Rosa?" Knight said, kissing her on the cheek as he walked past her and entered the house.

Rosa smiled at how take-control Knight had become with his boss-like attitude. She closed and locked the door behind him and then followed him into the front room. He then laid out stacks of money on to the coffee table.

"Knight, what's this?" she asked a bit confused.

"This is $20,000!" Knight told her, pushing the money across the table away from the rest of the cash. "Here's $100,000 more for five keys of coke. I want to get five instead of only another one."

Rosa was surprised, but she smiled at the young man's business savvy and actually respected him for his mind and style. She then sat down across from him.

"I see you're ready to move to the next level, but right now all I have are three keys left, Knight. I can sell you the three I have, and have five more when you're ready."

"Wait, make it ten!" he told her, with an expression on his face that showed her he was dead serious.

Rosa nodded her head and then said, "Ten it is then, Knight!"

Knight sat waiting while Rosa left to go and get the three bricks of coke that she had left for him. She returned a short time later with a black duffel back in her hand.

"Here you go, Knight," Rosa said, setting down the duffel bag on the coffee table in front of him.

"I'll see you soon, Rosa!" Knight told her as he stood up and picked up his backpack and the bag.

He then started toward the front door, with his mind already planning his next business moves.

Rosa followed Knight to the door and watched him as he walked out to his new SUV. She kept her eyes locked on the GMC Denali and watched as he pulled off, until he disappeared around the corner. She realized at that moment that she had made the wrong decision when trying to attach her niece to the young man. He needed a woman who was far above her niece's level—a woman who could match his level, which was certainly above a boy his own age. Rosa then shut the door and locked it, with a sneaky smile appearing on her face.

* * *

Karinne walked out of school after hearing the bell ring for lunch break. She walked out into the student parking lot with Gina and April. They passed by Eric with his new girlfriend, Tiffany, who was putting on a show by being all over Eric. Eric simply stood staring at Karinne with a smile on his lips, showing the wires that held his broken jaw in place. Karinne and her girls strolled over to where Duke was standing next to his Chevy Malibu along with two of his friends.

"Hey, baby!" April said as she walked up to Duke and kissed him on the lips.

"What up, y'all?" Duke said, nodding to both Karinne and Gina.

"Hey, Duke!" Gina said, smiling as she stood watching her girl and Duke.

"What's up, lover boy?" Karinne said with a smile. "How's the arm doing?"

"It's better!" Duke said as he used his good arm and reached over to rub his left arm. He then noticed Eric and his new lady walking their way. "Karinne, it looks like you have company."

Karinne looked in the direction Duke was looking and saw Eric and his girlfriend. She rolled her eyes as Eric and his bitch stopped within the group.

"What up, Duke?" Eric said, directing his attention to him. "I hear you the person to come see now! That true?"

"I'm lost, my nigga!" Duke replied, looking at Eric with an odd look. "What you trying to say?"

"Word is you're the one that's making the cash out there in them streets, and I'm trying to get my hands on some of that money. What I gotta do?"

"Try growing the fuck up!" Karinne said before she could stop herself.

"What, bitch?" Tiffany said as she turned to face Karinne. "I knew you ain't say shit to my man! I been waiting for a reason to beat your ass, hoe!"

"Act like it's your chance then, bitch!" April said as she dropped her books and stepped toward Tiffany, only for Karinne to grab her arm. "Naw, Karinne! This bitch needs to calm her ass down talking shit with them knock-off Louis Vuittons she's wearing. I'ma beat the bitch's ass!"

"April, chill!" Eric told her.

"Fuck you, nigga!" April went off. "Nigga, don't you say shit to me either with your punk ass. As a matter of fact, here comes my girl's man now. I wanna hear you talk that shit now, nigga!"

Eric saw that Karinne's man was indeed pulling into the parking lot. Knight had a grin on his face looking at his baby. Karinne stood watching the GMC Denali as it came to a stop where she and the others were standing.

"What up, y'all?" Knight called out after letting down his window and looking out.

"Boo, I think you need to straighten out this punk-ass nigga Eric!" April told Knight. "He out here disrespecting Karinne again."

"April!" Karinne yelled at the same time Knight swung open the driver's side door and attempted to get out.

Karinne rushed over to her man.

"Baby, relax. April's just talking shit again!"

"No I ain't!" April yelled out as Duke grabbed her arm and pulled her away from Eric and Tiffany.

"You always into something, girl," Duke told her as he dragged April over to where Knight and Karinne were standing.

Karinne stared at Knight as he stood watching Eric and Tiffany leave. She then reached up and gently turned his head to face her.

"Victor, I'm hungry. Can we go and get something to eat, please?"

"Sure!" Knight answered, gently brushing hair back out of her face.

He then bent down and kissed her on the lips.

Karinne quietly got caught up in the kiss with Knight. She put her arms around his neck as she ran her hands through his freshly done braids. She only broke the kiss when she and Knight heard April start in on them.

"Finally they ass get together, and now look at they ass! Can't stop with all the kissing and touching!" April exclaimed.

"Whatever!" Karinne cried while rolling her eyes playfully at April. "Baby, can we go now? I'm hungry."

"Yeah! Let's go, ma!" Knight told her, only for April and Gina to follow Karinne into the Denali.

Knight stopped Duke before he also climbed into the Denali.

"What's up, fam?" Duke asked, looking back at Knight after his boy stopped him. "Everything alright?"

"Everything's good," Knight answered. "We just need to talk later on after school."

"About?"

"Business."

"Say no more!" Duke said as he and Knight dapped up with each other before climbing into the SUV.

* * *

Knight and Duke were eating at the Golden Corral at the request of the girls, but they were mostly talking business the entire time. Knight broke down that they would be working with more dope than they had been before. He further explained that for now, he would be giving a key of coke to him and his cousins to push out on the streets at their same prices, but only pushing ounces on the streets.

After they had finished lunch and returned to school ten minutes before lunch break was over, Knight sat in the SUV while Karinne and the others stood outside talking and laughing. Knight pulled out the phonebook that belonged to Donavon, which was filled with the names of buyers.

Knight noticed that the words "minor" and "major" were printed in small lettering beside each name written in the book. He picked out a minor buyer by the name of Mr. Holmes and called the number. He listened to the line begin to ring, and someone picked up on the third ring.

"Hello!"

Knight spoke in the code Donovan had taught him, and he explained to Mr. Holmes everything he was told to say to the buyers in order to ensure to them who he was and with whom he was associated. Knight spent less than two minutes on the phone agreeing on a meeting location to further discuss business.

"Baby, you coming?" Knight heard, just as he was hanging up the phone. Karinne just stared at him.

Knight winked his eye at her, which caused her to smile. He then grabbed his backpack and climbed from the SUV.

ELEVEN

KNIGHT MET WITH MR. Holmes and got rid of two of the four bricks he was sitting on. He gave a brick to Duke and his cousins to put to work, and then connected with another one of Donavon's buyers, Mr. Showman, and got rid of the last brick. He had received a call from Rosa two days later letting him know that she was ready to meet with him concerning what the two of them had talked about.

Knight left school early the next day and made the drive out to Rosa's house to meet up about the ten bricks she was claiming to have ready. He parked his Denali out in front of the house and was climbing out of the SUV when he spotted her standing at the door wearing a silk robe.

"I figured you'd come by here today," Rosa stated, smiling as Knight walked up onto the porch.

She turned her head just as he was leaning in to kiss her on the cheek, only for their lips to meet for a brief moment before he stepped back.

"My fault, Rosa!" Knight apologized for the accident.

Rosa smiled when she saw Knight blush.

"It's perfectly fine, Knight. Come in!"

Knight stepped inside and caught the smell of perfume when he passed by her. He went into the front room but paused before he sat down, when he heard Rosa call out his name. He looked back to see Rosa motioning him to follow her as she headed to the back of the house.

"Back here, Knight!" she called, leading Knight into her bedroom.

She stopped at the door and waved him inside the room and then pointed to the duffel bag that was lying on top of her bed.

Knight tossed the backpack with the $200,000 inside onto the bed. He then opened the duffel bag and checked inside to see the ten bricks of cocaine.

"Knight, I've been meaning to tell you something," Rosa began as she walked up beside him and turned to face him. "I've really been watching you these last few months, and I've noticed the man you've become. You're not only a smart businessman, but you're an extremely handsome young man as well, and I respect how you've grown."

"Thanks, Rosa!" Knight told her, kissing her cheek and then turning to walk away, only for Rosa to grab his arm and pull him back around.

He was caught off guard when she kissed him directly on the lips and wrapped her arms around his neck.

Knight broke the kiss and gently moved Rosa back a few steps.

"Rosa, let's not do this. I respect and love Donavon too much to do this or anything to disrespect him in any way. We're also business associates, so we gonna act like this never happened," Knight respectfully explained.

Knight picked back up the duffel bag, left the bedroom, and headed toward the front door of the house, leaving Rosa in the bedroom with her face twisted up.

* * *

Knight dropped off the bricks at the stash apartment that he was able to get through a white male smoker to whom Melody had introduced him. He was on his way back to school when Melody called his phone.

"Yeah, Melody? What's up?"

"Knight, we got a problem! Cam'ron's teacher just called me at work."

"What happened, Melody?" Knight inquired, sighing as he began shaking his head.

"From what the teacher told me, your lil' man beat the mess out of one of the other students, Knight."

"You on your way to the school now?"

"Yeah! I can't be out long though, Knight. I gotta get back to work."

"Alright! I'ma meet you there."

After hanging up with Melody, Knight sent a quick text message to Karinne letting her know what was going on, and that he would be back at school to pick her up.

Knight arrived at the junior high school at which he was enrolled and parked his Denali. He then headed toward the front entrance of the school, entered, and walked straight toward the main office.

"Hello, sir!" the blonde white woman behind the front desk said with a smile as soon as she saw the handsome young man who entered the office.

"I'm here about my son!" Knight told her. "My wife was called and told that my son was involved in an altercation with another student."

"Would you be speaking about the young boy Cam'ron McKnight, sir?"

"That's correct!"

"Your wife is already here, sir!" the woman told Knight. "If you'll follow me, your wife and son are in the principal's office.

Knight followed the woman through the office to the principal's office. He stepped into the office after the woman knocked on the door and then opened it, announcing his arrival. Knight looked to his right and first laid eyes on Melody and then on Cam'ron. He balled up his face when he saw his little man's swollen eye and his busted lip.

"Mr. McKnight?" the principal asked as he stood up and offered his hand.

Knight shook the principal's hand and got straight into questioning the white man about his little man.

"What exactly happened to my son, and why exactly is he the one sitting in your office when it looks like my son is the one who was beat up?"

"Mr. McKnight, we've been trying to get Cam'ron to tell us exactly what happened, and he will not speak to me or your wife," the principal explained.

The principal began to continue, only for Knight to squat down beside Cam'ron.

"What happened, youngin?" Knight asked the boy, who looked up at him.

"I was jumped by these two boys because they wanted my Jordans and the chain you bought me. I got them back one by one and took my shoes and chain."

Knight nodded his head and rubbed Cam'ron's head as he stood back up and looked at the principal.

"Well, you got what you wanted, and my son just told you what happened. So now what?"

"Well, considering the damage your son caused to both boys, I'm forced to sus—!"

"Principal Bell!" Knight interrupted. "You drive a red Lexus, right?"

"How exactly do you know that, Mr. McKnight? Have we met before somewhere?" the principal asked surprised and confused.

"Actually, you've met business friends of mine who you've

done business with almost every Friday and Saturday, and sometimes Sunday over at the Cloverleaf Apartments," Knight informed the principal with a smirk on his face, knowing that the principal realized he was recognized. "I'm taking my son home for the rest of the day, but he'll be back tomorrow morning for school, correct?"

"Of course, he can return tomorrow morning, Mr. McKnight," the principal responded nervously.

Knight said nothing else to the principal, but he told Melody and Cam'ron that they were leaving. He followed them both out of the office, leaving the now sweating Principal Bell staring at their backs.

* * *

"I'm not going to ask what just happened back there, Knight!" Melody stated as she and Knight walked side by side into the parking lot while Cam'ron walked ahead of them.

"Good looking out for being there for me, Melody!" Knight told her as he hit the locks of his Denali by remote.

"Bye, Cam'ron!" Melody called out, waving bye to her baby with whom she was starting to fall in love. "You do know that boy is crazy about you, right?"

"That's my lil' man!" Knight said as he stopped at Melody's Cadillac CTS-V.

He then dug out a thick knot of money and peeled off $500 and handed it over to her.

"You bringing my baby over tonight, right?"

"I'ma hit you up when I'm on my way!" he told her, kissing Melody on the cheek and then turning and heading back over to his ride.

Knight climbed into the Denali and saw Cam'ron seated in the passenger seat with his head down. Knight started up the SUV and was backing out of the parking space when he asked the boy a question. "You hungry, youngin?"

"Yeah!" Cam'ron answered, and then wanted to know: "Knight, you mad at me?"

"For what, lil' man?"

"Because what I did!"

"Cam'ron, listen, lil' man!" Knight began, looking from the road over to the boy. "I can never be mad with you as long as what you was doing, or accused of doing, was in the right. But the only thing I want you to do is always think before you react to anything, because your decisions will affect how things could be later in life, whether it's bad or good. But this time, lil' man, I'm not mad at you! You handled your business!"

Seeing his little man smile at his words, Knight turned on the 26-inch Samsung monitor that was inside the dash, allowing Cam'ron to play with the PlayStation 4 that was connected to the monitor.

* * *

Knight returned to school just as Karinne and the others were getting out. He pulled up in front of the student parking lot entrance and hit the horn as he was letting down the window from the driver's side. He waved at Karinne when she spotted him. After getting her attention, Knight yelled out to Duke to get his attention, and then waved him over to his ride.

"What up, fam?" Duke said as he walked up to the driver's window and gave Knight a pound.

"Listen! I gotta handle something with my lil' man. But about the spot. How much of that left y'all holding?"

"He cool for maybe like two more days at the most!"

"Alright. I'ma get up with y'all later on after I see about the family."

"Do you, fam!" Duke told him as they dapped up again. "I got everything, bruh!"

Knight nodded his head as he put back up his window, and then he looked over toward Karinne.

"See about your family, huh?"

"That's what I said!" Knight said with a smile while he was driving off from in front of the school. "You is a part of this family, right?"

"Don't play with me, boy!" Karinne said as she playfully pushed him upside his head before turning her attention to Cam'ron in the back seat watching the monitor that flipped down from the ceiling of the Denali.

Knight picked up food for Karinne and her mother before pulling up in front of their house. Knight climbed out of the Denali and was walking around the front end of the SUV just as his cell phone began to ring inside his pocket. He dug out his iPhone as he followed Karinne and Cam'ron up to the front door, but he paused when he saw who was calling.

"Baby, what's wrong?" Karinne asked, after seeing the look on Knight's face.

Knight held up his hand for Karinne to hold on as he answered the phone.

"Stephen!"

"Knight!" he heard Stephen say before he went into a string of rapid Spanish that even Knight had a difficult time clearly understanding.

Knight hung up the phone and then looked at Karinne.

"Ma, I gotta go! I'll call you back in a few once I find out what's going on!"

"Victor!" Karinne yelled as he jogged back out to his truck.

Karinne could only stand and watch as Knight drove off, speeding up the block.

* * *

Duke made a sale of two ounces to a regular buyer that had been dealing with the team since shit first started up. He walked back over to the porch where his cousin Murphy and two new workers were posted. He slid the cash that he just made into his pocket, just as a new model F-150 pulled up.

"Yo, Murphy!"

Duke looked over at his cousin after his name was called out, and he saw him stand up from his seat and walk out to the truck. Duke dug out his ringing phone and sat down in Murphy's seat and saw that April was calling him.

"Yeah, April!"

"Baby, where you at now?"

"Where you think I'm at, girl? What's up, baby?"

"Duke, I need some money!" April told him. "I'm going to the mall with Gina and my cousin Tammy, and I need some money."

Duke sighed thinking about how fast Gina spent money. He told her that she had to wait or come by the spot to get the money, and he wasn't surprised when she told him that she was on her way. He hung up with her, only for the phone to ring again. Duke answered after seeing that Knight was on the other line.

"What up, fam?"

"Duke, I need you to drive out here to them old warehouses by I-95. You know where I'm talking about?"

"Yeah, sure!" Duke responded, already heading out to his car. "Is everything good though, fam?"

"Just get here!" Knight told him. "When you get here, drive

around to the back end and you'll see the Denali."

"I'm on my way now!" Duke said before hanging up the phone.

Duke yelled to his cousin to let him know that he was coming back later. He then hopped into the Malibu and was speeding away from the trap house moments later.

TWELVE

KNIGHT LEANED AGAINST THE wall next to the back entrance to the old furniture warehouse as he watched the Chevy Malibu pull up and park beside his Ford Explorer. Knight shifted his eyes back down to his phone as another text from Karinne came through. He read the message, just as Duke walked up the steps to where he stood.

"What's up, fam?" Duke asked as he pointed to the SUV. "Hey, ain't that Murphy's Explorer?"

"Pretty much!" Knight answered as he slid the iPhone back into his pocket. "Come on! Somebody wants to see you!"

Duke followed Knight into the warehouse, but he was confused about what was going on. He walked behind Knight until he first saw a shadow and then Stephen stepped into view.

"What the fuck!" he yelled in surprise almost pulling out his banger. "Where the fuck you been at, nigga?"

"He brought you a gift, fam!" Knight told Duke, nodding to his boy to keep following him until they walked farther out into an open area.

Knight then nodded toward a guy who was tied to a fold-out chair and had a hood over his head.

"That's for you right there, fam!"

Duke was confused as he looked from Knight to the guy who Knight pointed out, and then he glanced over at Stephen, who looked and smelled like shit. Duke walked over to the guy and kicked his foot, to which the guy cried out in terror.

"Who the fuck is this supposed to be?"

"Find out!" Knight told Duke, nodding for him to pull off the hood.

Duke turned back to the guy, reached out, and snatched the hood from his head.

"Oh shit!" Duke called out, seeing how fucked up homeboy looked.

"Dude look familiar, fam?" Knight asked.

"Familiar?" Duke asked, staring at the man's beaten face.

Knight started to tell Duke what he himself had just figured out: "That's the same person who was responsible for putting you in the hospital, fam! But it seems we have another problem."

"Fuck is you talking about?" Duke questioned while looking back over his shoulder at Knight.

"Our friend there wasn't just working by himself, fam," Knight began to explain. "It seems like we have a new friend that goes by the name of K.P. and he's the one that sent our friend there. But the hit was actually meant for me, and they thought you was me!"

"So what we doing, fam?" Duke asked, ready to let his hammer ring.

"First, we need to make a statement!" Knight told him, smiling as he began forming a plan inside his head.

But first, Knight needed to pay a visit to his mentor.

* * *

"Donavon King! You've got a visit!"

Donavon heard his name over the intercom and was surprised that he had a visitor. But he got up to get ready.

Five minutes later, he was escorted from his cell to the visitation room. Donavon entered the wing and walked down past two windows until he spotted his son leaning against the walls with his arms folded across his chest. Donavon then picked up the phone as he sat down on the table while watching Knight pick up the phone on his side of the window.

"What's up, youngin?"

"What's up, Pops?" Knight asked in reply. "How you doing in there? Has your lawyer come to see you?"

"He's looking into a few things for me because this case is real funny on a lot of levels. But what's up, youngin? You didn't come all the way out here to talk about my case. What's on your mind, Son?"

Donavon listened as Knight spoke in code telling him about how the attempt on Duke was actually meant for him, and how he also knew who was responsible for the hit attempt. Donavon waited until his son was finished speaking.

"So let me guess. You want me to tell you if you should go after this guy or not, right?" Donovan asked. "Don't look surprised, youngin! You remember I raised you, so I know how you think, boy!" Donavon said, seeing the look appear on Knight's face.

"So you think I should get at this dude then?" Knight asked.

Donavon thought a few moments and considered what was in front of him with everything Knight had told him. He then focused back on his son.

"Alright, youngin! If you're going to do this, then understand the problem you're up against. You may not believe it, but even inside here there's been a few guys talking about the young hustler that got at the dude Grip and his boy Terry. I remember you told me about that, but what you're planning to do now is on a totally different level. So we doing this right. Listen up real good, Son!"

Donavon spent the next fifteen minutes breaking down everything he wanted Knight to do once his son handled his business. Donavon then stood up from the table once the CO yelled that the visit was over.

"Remember what I told you, youngin!"

Donavon saw Knight nod his head in understanding. As he walked out of the visitation room, Donavon smiled proudly realizing how much Knight had grown.

* * *

Walking out of the jail after his visit with Donavon, Knight pulled out his phone and pulled up Duke's number.

"Yeah, fam!" Duke answered on the second ring.

"We all good, fam? Handle your business and make sure it's loud enough for everybody to see and understand."

"Not a problem!"

After hanging up with Duke, Knight started up his Denali and then pulled up Karinne's number.

"Hello!" Karinne answered sounding half-asleep.

"Ma, wake up!"

"What's wrong, baby? Where are you, Victor?"

"Where's Cam'ron?"

"He's asleep. Where are you?"

"I'm on my way to pick you up. Get something to wear for school tomorrow and pack a bag. You're coming to the apartment tonight with me and lil' man."

"How long before you get here?"

"About twenty minutes," he answered. "You hungry?"

"No, baby. Just hurry up, please!"

"I'm on my way."

After hanging up with Karinne, Knight then called Melody, hearing the phone ring twice before she picked up.

"Hello!"

"Melody, it's Knight."

"Hey, boy. What's up?"

"I'ma keep Cam'ron tonight, but you can pick him up from school tomorrow."

"Alright. Tell my baby I said I love him and will see him tomorrow."

"I'll tell him."

After hanging up with Melody, Knight tossed the phone onto the console. He turned up Notorious B.I.G.'s "No Beef" that was banging from his stereo.

* * *

Karinne received Knight's text message that he was pulling up outside. She woke up Cam'ron, and the both of them left her bedroom and headed for the front door. She got the little boy outside along with the bag she was carrying. She was just locking up the front door when the weight of her bag was lifted.

"Thank you!" she said with a smile as she kissed Knight, who stood holding Cam'ron and her bag.

Once Knight got out to his Denali, he buckled Cam'ron safely into the back seat, set Karinne's bag on the floor, and then walked around and sat behind the driver's seat. Karinne was already inside the SUV and was eating the fried fish and seasoned french fries Knight had picked up.

"I figured you were hungry," Knight said, smiling while she enjoyed the food he left for her on the seat.

"Here!" she said as she fed him a piece of fish.

Knight made the drive out to Oak Grove Apartment only stopping once for gas. He parked across the parking lot from his building and then got Cam'ron while Karinne climbed sleepily from the SUV with her bag. He led his family to his apartment. While still holding Cam'ron with one hand, he used his free one to unlock the door.

He locked the door behind them and then carried the boy to his bedroom. He undressed his little man down to his boxers and undershirt and then put him to bed. He smiled at how quickly the boy fell back asleep as soon as his head hit the pillow. Knight then left the bedroom and closed the door behind him.

Knight found Karinne already in the bed, but she was watching television. He set down his Glock on the dresser beside the bed and then began undressing down to his boxers and wifebeater.

"Cam'ron still asleep?" Karinne asked as she crawled over beside Knight and wrapped her arms across his middle as she laid her head on his chest.

"The boy is out!" Knight answered, wrapping his arm around Karinne and laying his hand on the curve of her butt. "Listen though, ma! I'm giving you the truck tomorrow because I've got something I need to take care of."

"So basically you're not coming to school with me, are you?" she asked as she lifted her head and rested her chin on his chest to look into his eyes.

"I've been thinking about that!" Knight stated. "I've decided to test for my GED."

"GED?"

"Yeah!"

"So you're dropping out of school, Victor?"

"Naw, ma! I'm just finishing a year earlier than I would be if I stayed in for my senior year. What's wrong with a GED?"

"Baby, there's nothing wrong with a GED. A lot of very important and famous people have one, but I was looking forward to us finishing together, that's all!"

Victor sighed as he pulled Karinne over on top of him. He then wrapped his arms around her back while meeting and holding her eyes.

"Kay, you know I love you, right?"

"I love you too!"

"I promise on my very life that as long as I breathe and have an able body, we'll be together and you'll never have to want for nothing. I swear it!" he made a promise to her and meant every word that left his lips.

Karinne held her man's beautiful eyes and saw the seriousness inside. She kissed his lips but then sat up and straddled him. She pulled off the long T-shirt she had on, allowing her braless C-cup breasts to spill out.

"Make love to me, Victor!" she told him, bending back down to passionately kiss his lips.

THIRTEEN

KNIGHT HEARD HIS CELL phone vibrate from over on top of his dresser while Karinne slept beside him. He picked up the phone and saw an incoming text message. It was the message he had been waiting on. He climbed from the bed and saw that Karinne was still sleeping. He quickly got dressed in all-black jeans, a T-shirt, and black Tims that he stepped into. Knight grabbed his keys and Glock, but he removed the spare key and laid it down beside Karinne's cell phone before kissing her on the cheek and heading toward the bedroom door. He grabbed his black leather jacket from behind the door on his way out.

Knight locked up his apartment behind him once he stepped outside. He then walked out into the parking lot and saw Stephen behind the wheel of the Audi Ayisha drove.

"What up?" Knight asked as he climbed into the Audi.

"Everything's set up!" Stephen said as he pulled off.

Knight nodded his head in reply before breaking his silence.

"What's up with, Ayisha?"

"Rosa sent her back to Puerto Rico!" Stephen told him, stopping from saying anything else since there was no point.

Both of them remained silent and in their own thoughts on different things with which they were each dealing. Stephen then turned the Audi into the parking lot of a farm store while Murphy, Sean, and Duke were waiting inside Murphy's Explorer. Knight let down his window as Stephen pulled up alongside the Explorer on the passenger side where Duke sat.

"What's up, fam?" Duke said, leaning out the window a little to speak with Knight.

"Tell me, what's the deal with this clown?" Knight asked Duke, taking the blunt that he passed over to him.

"Dude lives with baby momma and his daughter," Duke began. "Right now though, it's him and three other dudes up in his house. I ain't sure where the baby momma and shorty are though!"

"Where's ol' boy at who pulled the hit for this clown?" Knight asked when he saw Duke nod to the back seat of the Explorer.

"Sean's watching his ass, fam!" Duke stated as he looked back to Sean with the supposed hit man.

"Alright!" Knight said, looking over at Stephen and seeing his boy calmly staring straight ahead out the front windshield.

"Let's get this over with!" Knight said as he looked back at Duke.

* * *

K.P. laughed as he stood up from his spot on the sofa and handed a blunt over to his boy Ken before he stepped by Bull. He walked over to the front door still laughing at the old-school *Eddie Murphy Raw* video they were watching. He unlocked the front door, but he was so focused on watching the television that he barely got out of the way when the body fell on top of him.

"What the fuck!" K.P. yelled, leaping backward just as the body fell to the floor.

"What the hell!" Ken exclaimed as he, Bull, and Rick rushed over beside K.P.

"Who the fuck is that?" Bull asked as Ken turned the body over.

"Oh shit!" Rick yelled, instantly recognizing the face of the body laid in front of him and his boys. "That's that nigga L.B.!"

"Yeah! That's the same name he gave me!" K.P. and his boys heard as they looked up to see five young boys standing just inside his front door, each of them with a banger or two in their hands.

"Fuck!" K.P. said, recognizing the light-skinned kid with the long braids.

"It's good to see that you recognize me now!" Knight stated with a small smile on his face as he stared at K.P, whom he remembered seeing a few times before. "I hear you was looking for me but found my brother. I decided to just drop in and visit. Stephen!"

Boom! Boom! Boom! Boom! Boom!

Knight watched as Stephen let off rounds into each of K.P.'s homeboys, bodying each of them. Knight called to Murphy and Sean, who rushed K.P. and began beating the shit out of the boy. He allowed it to continue a few minutes.

"That's enough, fellows! Let's get the fuck outta this shit! Duke, go ahead and burn this shit to the ground!"

They all turned and exited the house, with Murphy half-dragging a knocked-out K.P. from inside.

* * *

Knight and Stephen took K.P. to the same warehouse where they had taken L.B. They both stood watching as first Duke and then Sean and Murphy beat K.P. to sleep, only to wake his ass up just to beat him back to sleep again. Knight let the beating go on until Duke and his cousins were tired and covered in blood and sweat. He stopped his boys and then looked at Stephen, who nodded in understanding. He then walked from beside him and approached K.P.

"What you plotting on now, fam?" Duke asked out of breath as he pulled off his bloody and sweaty shirt. "We murdering this fool or what?"

"Pretty much!" Knight answered. "But we not just killing this fool. We're making a statement with this clown for the whole city to know that you don't fuck with us!"

Knight swung his head around just as both Sean and Murphy turned around as well when they all heard the terrifying scream coming from K.P. Stephen had taken a knife to the boy's throat, hacking at it until the whole damn head came the fuck off and blood shot up like a waterfountain. Duke just shook his head.

"Damn!"

"This dude is crazy as fuck!" Sean said as he stood staring at Stephen holding K.P.'s head with a devilish-looking smile on his crazy muthafucking face.

* * *

They relocated K.P.'s body and left it inside the busiest part of the city, to make certain the body would be quickly found once the city woke up. Knight and Stephen drove back out to the stash apartment while Duke and his cousins followed behind them.

"What's the plan now, hermano?" Stephen asked, glancing over at Knight.

"We relocate for a little while!" he told Stephen, seeing the surprised expression that shot across his boy's face. "Relax! We're not running, but laying low for a few weeks or more. After what we just did, the city is going to be on fire with people trying to figure out who's responsible for what we did to K.P. I'm mostly concerned about the police flooding the streets and asking questions and looking all over the place. It's best if we just get ghost for a while!"

"So where we going then?" Stephen asked him.

"Kissimmee!" Knight responded, thinking about the friend Donavon had out that way to whom he was supposed to reach out.

Knight made it back to the stash apartment and got his team all inside the same room. He then broke down the news on how things were going to play out. He first explained to Duke that he, Stephen, and himself were leaving town for a while to handle business as well as to lay low until things cooled off after K.P.'s body was discovered. Knight then addressed Sean and Murphy and explained to them that he was entrusting the business to them. However, he made it clear that they would continue to take orders from either him or Duke by phone. Knight also explained that they were not to make any major decisions without discussing them with him and Duke first.

"What about work?" Sean interrupted.

"I'm leaving two bricks with you two, along with the rest of what you both got left," Knight told them, looking from Sean and Murphy. "Every two weeks, you both should be finished with the two bricks and ready to re-up. Either Duke or myself will meet up with you two in Orlando, and I'll have two more bricks for y'all to take back with you to Miami."

"So how long y'all gonna be gone?" Murphy asked him.

"No longer than two months!" Knight answered, making the decision on the spot.

After finishing up the meeting with his crew by the time the sky was getting light, Knight and Stephen headed out to the Audi, when Duke called out to Knight as he jogged out to catch up with his boy.

"Fam, I was wondering. We taking the girls with us, right?" Duke asked Knight.

"Naw, fam!" Knight told him. "We not taking the girls, because even though we leaving Miami, this is still business. I'm not even telling Karinne where we going, but I'ma have someone let her know I'll be gone for a while."

"You know she's gonna wild out about it once she finds out, right?" Duke said.

"She'll be alright!" Knight told Duke as the two of them gave each other a pound. "We'll meet at the Shell gas station on County Line Road down the 441."

"What time?"

"We'll meet in one hour," Knight replied as he followed Stephen out to the Audi.

* * *

By the time Knight returned to his apartment, he knew Karinne had already left for school since the Denali was gone. He packed a light bag and decided he would do some shopping once he got to Kissimmee. He left the apartment a few minutes later and climbed back inside the Audi, where he saw Stephen on the phone.

Knight caught on to the conversation Stephen was having in Spanish with Rosa. They were arguing about loyalty to his family, when, in fact, his family didn't give a fuck about him. Knight also caught Stephen's comment about his loyalty and devotion to his brother—and only his brother.

Knight saw Stephen angrily hang up the phone on Rosa. He then cut his eyes back over to his boy as Stephen drove with his face showing his anger.

"I ain't know you also had a brother, playboy!"

"You're my only hermano!" Stephen stated as he looked from the road over to meet Knight's eyes.

Knight nodded his head in full understanding and then focused his attention elsewhere. But he could feel the loyalty from his brother/hermano sitting beside him.

FOURTEEN

KNIGHT LEFT MIAMI BY 8:30 a.m. and made the two-hour drive out to Kissimmee by 11:00 a.m. He headed straight to Gaylord Palms Resort, which was the hotel Donavon had told him about. Knight, Stephen, and Duke walked out of the filled parking lot and entered the high-rise hotel.

"What the fuck!" Duke said once he stepped into the hotel behind Stephen.

He looked around and thought the lobby looked like a mini city. He was caught up by the interior, and then looked up to see the glass dome overhead.

"Yo, Duke!" Stephen called, getting Duke's attention and waving him over.

Knight shook his head and smirked when he saw the look on Duke's face, but he was just as impressed with the place himself. Knight then turned his attention back to the front desk, just as a white couple in front of them had finished up.

"Good morning, gentlemen," the red-headed front desk clerk said, smiling at the three handsome young men. "How can I help you three today?"

"We would like three rooms, please," Knight stated as he dug his hand into his pocket.

"We have a different level of rooms, sir."

"Three penthouse suites will do!" Knight interrupted her as he held out a large knot of money in his fist. "Make sure all three rooms are on the same floor, please."

"Not a problem, sir," she replied, looking at Stephen and then back to Knight. "And, sir, our penthouse suites are $2,500 a night, and we do not take cash, only some form of credit card or debit card, sir."

"Ummm," Knight began, trying to think since he didn't carry plastic. "Is there somewhere around here where I can buy a debit card?"

"Actually, sir, we have many places here at Gaylord Palms," the clerk told Knight with a smile.

* * *

About ten minutes after buying four debit cards and putting $5,000 on each one, Knight handed a card over to Stephen and Duke and kept two for himself. He paid for the suites, and then the three of them rode the glass elevator up to the forty-seventh floor, on which the penthouse suites were located.

Knight tossed a key card over to Stephen and another one to Duke as they made their way into their own rooms. He then used his card and entered his suite, which looked like a mini apartment once he stepped inside. He chuckled lightly to himself as he began looking around the suite. After admiring the nice-sized kitchen, he made his way to the bedroom, which had a big-ass bed in the middle.

"Nice!"

Knight dropped his bag onto the bed as he walked around to the phone that lay atop the bedside table. He picked it up as he dug out the paper on which he wrote the contact number of Donavon's friend. He then dialed the number and stood and listened to the line ring until it was picked up.

"*Hola*!"

Knight spoke in Spanish and asked to speak with Ramos Ramirez after introducing himself over the phone.

"I've been waiting for your call!" Ramos told Knight in English. "This is Ramos. Donavon told me you would be contacting me soon. Are you in Kissimmee yet?"

"I'm actually at the Gaylord Palms Resort."

"I know exactly where that's at!" Ramos said, cutting him off. "How about this, Victor? I'll meet you out at the hotel, and we can have dinner and talk a little."

"That'll work!"

"Great! Give me twenty minutes and I'll be there!"

"Cool!"

After hanging up the phone with Donavon's homeboy, Knight then called Duke to let him know what was happening. He expressed that he was okay for Duke to hang back or do whatever while he met up with Ramos. Knight hung up and then called Stephen, but they had a different conversation.

"*Hola*!"

"It's Knight, bruh!"

"What's up, hermano?"

"We're having a visitor in twenty minutes."

"I'll be downstairs in fifteen minutes."

Once Stephen hung up the phone, Knight could only smile as he laid down the headset and then got up to get ready for his meeting.

* * *

Knight showered and dressed in a casual Gucci outfit and some suede Gucci loafers. He rode the elevator back down the floors to the lobby, stepped off once the doors opened, and then walked over to the front desk. He spoke with a clerk and asked if anyone had stopped by looking for him.

"Your name, sir?" the male desk clerk requested.

"Victor McKnight," Knight stated as he stood a few moments until the clerk looked from the computer back up to him. "I don't see any messages, but please wait a moment and I'll check if you have any written messages."

Knight nodded in agreement and turned around to see if Stephen was in the lobby yet. He thought he spotted his boy, when someone crossed his line of view and stopped at the front desk beside him. He stood staring at the red-bone and slim but curvy female with perky breasts. She had a nice rounded and high ass that fit perfectly inside the jeans she was wearing. Knight caught and held her hazel brown eyes after she brushed back some of her shoulder-length raven-black hair from her face.

"Mr. McKnight, sir!" Knight heard someone call out, which caused him to break eye contact and look back toward the desk clerk.

"You do have one message, sir," the clerk informed Knight and then handed him a folded note.

Knight thanked the young man behind the desk and accepted the note. He looked back to his left but wasn't surprised to see that the female was gone. He shook his head as he turned his attention down to the note. After reading the message, he balled up the paper and then turned around to look for The Steakhouse.

* * *

"Bingo!" Ramos exclaimed as he broke out into a smile while seated at a table in the restaurant.

He spotted the young man who was described to him, and realized how accurate his friend Donavon was about him. Ramos stood up, waved his hand, and called out, "Knight!" Ramos got Knight's attention and waved him over. He remained standing as Knight walked up to the table. He then held out his hand to the young man. "It's good to finally meet you, Victor Knight."

"It's Victor McKnight," he corrected the brown-skinned Spaniard. "I'm called Knight though, so you're good!"

Ramos smiled as he motioned for Knight to take a seat. Ramos adjusted his seat and was just about to say something, when he heard some minor commotion.

"Umm, is he with you?"

Knight looked back in the direction Ramos was staring and instantly spotted Stephen about to act up as three employees stopped him from entering the restaurant.

"That's my brother!" Knight admitted as he shook his head and smirked.

Ramos stood up again and called out to one of the employees who was having a difficult time with Knight's brother. He then pointed to the young man and motioned for his release. Ramos pulled over a chair from another table and sat back down.

When Stephen walked over to the table, he and Knight nodded at one another. Stephen then removed the chair Ramos had brought to their table and set it back at the other table, where he took a seat.

"Interesting young man!" Ramos stated with a smile as he nodded over at Stephen. "I was surprised when Donavon called and told me that he was locked up. I know of you already, but it came as a surprise to me when he recently called to let me know that you were moving down to Kissimmee for some time. I was told that with your new power down in Miami, you also gained a few problems that you were forced to deal with!"

"That may be so, but business doesn't stop!" Knight explained with a face that showed his seriousness.

Ramos smiled upon hearing the statement made by Knight.

"You sound exactly like Donavon. It's clear you are his son!"

Switching gears, Knight turned to business talk.

"Donavon tells me there's money out here, and more than enough that I can get some!"

"What exactly are you trying to get into?" Ramos asked as he sat back in his chair, folded his hands in front of him, and held Knight's eyes.

"I'm looking to reach out and spread the love! You get what I'm saying?"

"Of course!" Ramos replied. "I can introduce you to a lot of people! I'm well known in this—!"

"Whoa!" Knight interrupted him. "I hear what you saying, but I come bearing gifts of my own!"

"Well, since you've made that known, I can introduce you to some potential buyers you can connect with!"

Knight nodded his head and listened to Ramos continue their conversation until a server arrived to take their orders. Knight ordered first, followed by Ramos, and then he announced to the server that the young man at the table next to them was also with their group. Once the server was finished and had left their table, Ramos then focused back onto Knight.

"There's something going on out at this club in downtown Orlando by the name of Firestone. We can go there and I can begin introducing you to some people, but tomorrow afternoon I'm also throwing a cookout at my place, and you'll meet more people there!"

"Yeah! That'll work!" Knight stated as he immediately began planning and plotting his next moves.

IFTEEN

KARINNE WAS PAST BEING upset and was now pissed the hell off, since her supposed boyfriend still had not called to let her know where the hell he was or why he even left without telling her. She sat on her bed at her mother's house after leaving Knight's apartment. She had received a call from Melody, who Karinne had no idea who she was, and was told that Knight would call her once he got settled where he was going. She was also told that Knight wouldn't allow Melody to tell Karinne where he was, but that he would explain when his ass called, which she was still waiting for.

"This muthafucker better have a great—!" Karinne started as she snatched up her ringing cell phone, but never finishing what she was saying. "Victor, this better be you, nigga!"

"Girl, no!" April said, sucking her teeth. "I see Victor's ass ain't called you either. I'm waiting on Duke to call me back, and his ass still hasn't."

"Hold on!" Karinne yelled. "You mean Duke actually did call you already?"

"Yeah! His ass called, but I missed the call!"

"You called him back yet?"

"He left a message saying he would call me later, and that he was getting rid of his phone, but that he was getting a new one."

"So that explains why his ass can't be reached!" Karinne said in understanding. "Victor is really pushing his luck with this shit!"

"Duke's ass also!" April agreed, giving an attitude. "I know one thing though. Let me find out Duke's ass is with the next bitch, and I promise, Karinne, I am going to really hurt that nigga! He better not try me!"

"You think Duke and Victor would try something like that?" Karinne asked, already thinking in that direction but trying not to think like that about the man with whom she was in love.

"Truthfully, Karinne, I love Duke, but I really don't know what to think right now. I know if I find out something I don't like, I'm going to jail, and I mean it!"

* * *

"This is what the fuck I'm talking about!" Duke said as he leaned over toward Knight as he, Knight, Stephen, and Ramos all entered the packed club called Firestone.

Knight smirked after hearing the excited tone in Duke's voice, but he kept his eyes moving as Ramos led the way through the club. He heard people yelling out to Ramos from every direction. Knight then spotted a few of the people that called out to Ramos, and caught their stares before they looked on.

"Double R?"

Ramos heard the nickname that most guys called him, and he looked over to his left and saw Jonathan Sanchez and his boy Cristan

Santana heading his way. Ramos then leaned toward Knight.

"These two right here walking up are two guys I want you to consider dealing with."

"Double R, what up?" Jonathan said as he and Ramos embraced.

"How you guys doing?" Ramos stated as he embraced Cristan.

"What's been going on?" Jonathan asked before he switched to Spanish and explained that he and Cristan had been trying to connect on some business.

"I've been busy!" Ramos started, and then quickly introduced Knight. "But I got somebody I want you boys to meet. This is my boy Donavon's son, Knight."

"You Donavon's boy?" Both Jonathan and Cristan asked at the same time while looking over Knight.

"You Spanish?" Jonathan asked Knight, staring hard at his facial features.

"*Puertorriqueño* and *negro*," Knight explained in Spanish, letting both guys know he was Puerto Rican and black.

"Fellas, look!" Ramos spoke up again. "I'm having a cookout tomorrow at my house. How about you two come over?"

"We're there!" Jonathan replied before he looked at Knight and shook up with him. "Make sure you tell King that Jonathan and Cristan said what's up!"

"I'll be around a while, but next time I talk to him I'll tell him," Knight told the two guys before they walked off.

Knight continued to follow Ramos and then asked, "What's up with those two?"

"Who? Jonathan and Cristan?" Ramos asked. "They used to do a few jobs for Donavon, and Donavon used to deal with them with business as well."

"What you mean jobs?" Knight asked as three women stopped by and hugged Ramos one by one.

Ramos smiled as he watched the women walk on, and then he looked over at Knight shaking his head.

"Those two play both sides of the game. They sell, but they're mostly hired guns!"

Knight nodded his head in understanding, and then made a mental note to get back with both Jonathan and Cristan.

Knight continued to follow Ramos through the club and meet more people who caught and held his attention, and whom he planned on speaking with again. He was really interested in the older Cuban guy who Ramos introduced as Juan who was sitting inside the VIP section. He spoke with the arrogant Cuban for only a short time, but he made sure to learn as much as he could in those few minutes. Knight knew he would be speaking with the Cuban again very soon. He then followed Ramos out of VIP and back to the bar, where they ordered drinks.

"So, what do you think?" Ramos asked once he, Knight, and Knight's friends all had drinks in their hands.

Knight heard Ramos's question, but he was too busy looking in on someone familiar and of interest.

"Fam, what up?" Duke asked Knight, who was staring in another direction.

"Huh!" Knight asked, really not paying attention to what Duke had just said, but watching the same red-bone girl from back at the hotel lobby he saw earlier.

Knight was caught up looking over her 36-28-40, 5'10" frame as she smoothly moved to the music out on the dance floor with two other females dancing together.

Knight slowly smiled while watching her move, and then he peeped the guy that slipped up behind the girl and began grinding up against her ass. He caught the look she shot back at the guy over her shoulder before she began trying to pull away from him. Knight then watched as the guy grabbed hold of her waist and began grinding harder on her.

* * *

Kia forced the guy off of her and then spun around and slapped the shit out of him while he was grinding his dick all on her butt. She swung around again and slapped him again; only this time the guy slapped her back, knocking her to the floor.

"Bitch! You the—!"

"Hell naw!" Kia yelled as she jumped up from the floor and attacked the guy, swinging at him and trying to claw his eyes out.

"Whoa!" someone yelled as they grabbed her around the waist and lifted her off her feet, turning her away from the homeboy she was fucking up.

"Let me the fuck go!" Kia yelled, fighting to get free from whomever was now holding her.

She wanted to get back to the asshole that was disrespecting her and had put his hands on her.

"Watch the fuck out, nigga!" the guy yelled.

But the guy made the mistake of laying his hands on Knight, only for seconds to pass when he felt a bottle smash across his head, knocking him to the floor.

Knight watched as Duke busted homeboy upside the head with his Heineken bottle as the crowd pushed through to get to where the action was. Knight instantly peeped the vibe and placed the female behind him. He then turned to face the crowd of eight guys, just as Stephen stepped onto the scene with his hand tucked up underneath his shirt front.

"Muthafucker, you just signed your papers that say you ready to die!" one of the eight guys said as two others helped their homeboy from the ground.

"I tell you and your boys what!" Knight said with a smirk, knowing that things were about to get real interesting. "Your boy fucked up, and he paid for it; now you and your boys can leave or we can yellow tape this whole club. You niggas decide!"

"Decide fast!" Jonathan yelled as he and Cristan pushed through the crowd to stand with Knight and his boys.

Knight smirked harder when their faces changed from pissed off to worried. He then saw two more guys step up, who Ramos had introduced to him earlier as Javier and Alex.

"What up, Knight? Jonathan, do we got a problem here, my nigga?" Javier asked, with his New York accent as he and his main man Alex stood to the right of the eight guys.

Knight chuckled and then looked back at the eight guys and saw that their worried expressions had now turned into ones of fear. He spoke up once more.

"Last chance! Take your boy on up out of here, y'all, or we can start redecorating this place right now. Decide now, playboy!"

* * *

Knight chopped it up with Jonathan, Cristan, Alex, and Javier after homeboy and his crew left. Knight introduced Stephen and Duke to the four hired killers and businessmen. He then peeped Ramos walking up and smiling as he felt a tap on his shoulder.

"I guess I owe you a thank you!" Kia said with a slight smile, now remembering that she saw him at the Gaylord Palms and learned his name was Knight.

"Naw!" Knight answered, smiling as he held the female's eyes. "I just saw what was going down, and didn't want homeboy to mess up that pretty face!"

Kia blushed as she smiled. She then remembered her girls and introduced Lena and Erica to Knight.

"What's your name though?" Knight asked while smiling down at her.

"It's Kia!" she told him, still smiling. "What about you, or is Knight your real name?"

"It's short for McKnight, but that's my last name, ma. It's actually Victor, but everyone calls me Knight."

"I like Knight better."

"Make sure you use it then!" Knight told her, still flirting lightly with Kia.

Knight continued to talk with Kia and then introduced her and her friends to Stephen, Duke, and the others. He would have kept talking to her, but Ramos interrupted to let him know that it was time for them to leave.

Recognizing the warning, Knight got Kia to write down her number and then promised to call her. He and his team then turned and all headed toward the exit.

* * *

"I see you make friends easily!" Ramos said to Knight.

Ramos, Knight, Duke, and Stephen all left the club together and then got into Ramos's Cadillac Escalade Premium. Although Knight heard Ramos's comment, he chose not to respond to it.

"Tell me about Jonathan, Cristan, Alex, and Javier," Knight

asked Ramos.

"What's to tell?" Ramos replied. "Didn't you see how everybody reacted when not just Jonathan and Cristan but also Alex and Javier showed up? Those four are known killers and dope boys, and even businessmen worry when those four show up. Javier and Jonathan are cousins, so they're always seen together. But Jonathan works with Cristan and has since they were young boys. They are about your age now and wild as hell, but they also mess around in the drug game while Alex and Javier deal with robbing and putting people to sleep forever."

Knight nodded his head after listening to Ramos.

"I need you to make sure these four are at the party tomorrow. I've got a plan for each of them."

"Consider it done!" Ramos stated with a smile on his lips.

"One more thing!" Knight spoke up again. "I wanna pick up another ride."

"We'll take care of it tomorrow morning," Ramos answered. "I know a few dealership owners. You like Mercedes?"

"That'll work," Knight responded as he stared out of his window from the passenger side deep in thought plotting and planning.

* * *

Once they were all back at the hotel and inside his suite, Knight went over his plans with Duke and Stephen, since he wanted them all to be on the same page. He was very happy to see that his boys were ready to ride with him with his plans. Knight kicked it with his guys a little while longer until he remembered that he needed to call Karinne, even though it was quite late by then.

After Duke and Stephen left his suite, Knight put a shower on hold and lay across the bed and called Karinne's cell phone, only to end up listening to the line until it went directly to voicemail. He hung up and tried calling the number again, but ended up getting her voicemail again and just leaving her a message.

Knight set down the phone after leaving a message for Karinne. He was just about to get up from the bed when his suite phone rang, so he picked it up.

"Hello!"

"Is this Victor McKnight?"

Knight balled up his face hearing the question and the use of his full name.

"Who the fuck is this?"

"Wow! Somebody instantly got on their guard at the use of their name!" the caller said with a giggle. "Relax, Knight. This is Kia!"

Knight sighed softly, but he was pretty sure that she heard him since she began to laugh. In turn, Knight began to laugh himself.

"I see you like to play, huh?"

"A little! You busy?"

"I was about to jump in the shower, but I'll talk for a few minutes."

"I feel special now!" she told Knight jokingly. "So tell me, Knight. Where are you from? You've got an up-North accent, but you dress like a down-South guy."

"I'm actually from Flint, Michigan, but I moved to Miami with my pops and his girl."

"What part of Miami you from, Knight?"

"Why? You thinking about visiting after I leave?"

"Maybe!" she answered. "But for real. I'm from Miami and just moved out here!"

"My pops bought our house in the Norwood area, and I went to Miami Norland Senior High School.

"Boy, I stayed right there in Miami Gardens, and I went to Norland as well," she told him while laughing. "Maybe if I ran into you, I would have stayed in Miami instead of coming this way."

"Oh really?" Knight asked, smiling as he lay back across the bed.

"How old are you, Knight?"

"I'm seventeen now. My birthday just passed the day before yesterday."

"I'm a year older than you!" she told him. "So do you have a woman, Knight?"

Knight immediately lost his smile when he thought about Karinne. He sighed loudly, but he was truthful with Kia.

"Actually, I do, and I think I owe you an apology because I'm doing a lot of flirting. I won't lie and say I'm not attracted to you, because I am; but I wasn't thinking about my lady when you and I met. I'm sorry!"

"I'm not!" Kia admitted. "I'm attracted to you as well, but I will respect that you belong to another woman. Can we at least be friends, Knight?"

"Yeah! That'll work for me, ma!" he answered with a big grin.

"I'm happy to hear that!" she told him sighing. "So tell me, gorgeous. What's the girl's name who was lucky enough to get you?"

"Karinne!" Knight told her with a smile.

"Wait!" Kia said. "You say Karinne, right?"

"Yeah! Why?"

"Is her full name Karinne King, Knight?"

"How you know that? You know Karinne, ma?"

Kia laughed at what was happening and then said, "This is a small damn world. I actually know Karinne real well, even though we really didn't talk or hang together. I still know her or of her!"

"Well, damn!" was the only thing Knight could think to say after hearing how fucked up his luck was.

SIXTEEN

KNIGHT AND STEPHEN WERE up early and dressed by the time Ramos called to say that he was waiting down in the parking lot of the hotel. The two young men stopped to pick up Duke in his suite. He was just getting off the phone with April, who was yelling over the phone. The three rode the elevator down to the lobby and headed out the front entrance, where they saw Ramos parked in front in a Land Rover Range Rover.

"What's up, fellas?" Ramos asked with a smile as Knight and his boys climbed into the SUV. "We've got an appointment with a friend of mine."

"Appointment?" Knight asked, looking over at Ramos.

"My friend that works at the dealership," Ramos informed them. "I called and spoke with him last evening and explained that I had family in town and that I was bringing the three of you out to see him."

Knight nodded his head after listening to Ramos. He then mentioned that he needed Ramos to take him, Duke, and Stephen to get new cell phones, to which Ramos expressed that he'd take care of it.

Knight, Stephen, Duke, and Ramos arrived at the Mercedes-Benz dealership about fifteen minutes later. They all climbed from the Range Rover as soon as Ramos parked, and the three of them started toward the show lot. Ramos smiled after climbing from his SUV, and saw Knight leading his boys through the sea of cars and SUVs. Ramos locked up and then started toward the dealership's front entrance to look for his friend.

* * *

"McKnight!"

Knight heard his name being called as he, Stephen, and Duke stood looking at a dark indigo, new-model Mercedes-Benz G63. Knight turned around to see Ramos and a blonde-haired white boy wearing glasses walking toward them. He then looked back at the Benz SUV as Ramos and the salesperson reached them.

"McKnight, this is the guy I told you about," Ramos began. "Aaron Peters, this is my nephew, Victor McKnight."

"Have you gentlemen found anything you like?" Aaron asked as he stepped up beside Knight.

"I want this one!" Knight replied, looking back at the Benz SUV and then over to the salesperson.

"The G63!" Aaron repeated with a smile on his face.

The salesman was just about to say more, only to be interrupted by Knight.

"Listen, Peters. I don't want to hear the sales pitch! I want the G-Wagen, and then you can take care of my brothers, and they will tell you what they want. Then I want you to get the paperwork taken care of, because we've got other things we need to get done!"

* * *

"Hi, Daddy!" Karinne said, smiling at her father through the thick glass window in the visitation room of the jail.

"Hey, baby girl!" Donavon responded, returning the smile for his daughter. "What are you doing out here by yourself when Knight is out of town?"

"I'm not out here by my—! Wait!" Karinne cried, after realizing what her father just said. "Daddy, how do you know Victor is out of town?"

"That's not important, Karinne."

"Yes it is!" Karinne cried out. "How is it that you and whoever this bitch Melody is that called me about Victor know where my man is, and I don't?"

"Karinne, I understand that!"

"You can't understand nothing!" Karinne yelled and cut off her father. "Victor just up and left without telling me shit, and now you're with the games he's playing. It's alright. I'ma teach him about playing with me!"

Donavon watched as his daughter slammed down her phone, jumped out of her seat, and walked off from the visitation window. Donavon shook his head as he hung up his phone and then stood up from his seat. He then called out for the guard to come get him and take him back to his room.

* * *

Once Donavon returned to his cell, he went directly to the phone area. He stood with his back against the wall looking out over the day room floor while listening to the phone line ring. He then heard Melody finally answer the line and accept the call.

"Hello!"

"What's up, lady?"

"You tell me! I was coming to see you later this afternoon."

"Still come. I wanna see you. But listen, baby. Has my son contacted you with his new number yet?"

"He actually just called me. I just hung up with Knight after he spoke with Cam'ron for a little while. Everything alright?"

"Call the boy for me, Melody."

"Hold on!"

Donavon waited a few moments while Melody set up a three-way call with Knight. Donavon heard the sound of his voice just as Melody clicked back over.

"Hey, Knight!" Melody said in greeting. "Donavon's on the phone for you."

"Pops, what's up?"

"How's it going, youngin?" Donavon asked with a smile when he heard his son's voice. "Sounds like you already setting up out there."

"I'm getting it together! What's up though, old man?"

"When's the last time you talked with Karinne, youngin?"

"I tried calling her last night after I got back to the hotel. Why?"

"I just got a visit from her, and my advice to you is to call her, Son. She's pissed and talking about teaching you a lesson."

"I'm on it, Pops!"

"Good!" Donavon began. "But one more thing. Our message you left before you went to handle other business was heard loud and clear, youngin."

"Just let me know when, and I'm on my way back home!"

"You'll know when, youngin."

* * *

After hanging up with Melody and Donavon, after receiving the message concerning Karinne, Knight was just about to pull up her number, when his phone rang with Stephen's number and name across the screen.

"Yeah!"

"Hermano, we've got a problem!"

"Talk about it!"

"Not over the phone."

"Alright!" Knight said as he hit the horn on his new G-Wagen to get Ramos's attention and motioned him to pull over.

Knight saw Ramos pull over into the parking lot of a BP gas station, so he turned the G-Wagen into the gas station behind the Land Rover. He climbed out of his new SUV just as Duke was turning in behind him in his new Benz E350 drop-top. Stephen followed right behind in his new E-Class Benz.

"What's the problem?" Ramos questioned as he left his SUV and walked up right beside Knight.

"I'm about to find out now!" Knight informed him, just as Stephen and Duke walked up. "What's good, Steph?"

"Hermano, it's Rosa!" he began. "She's pissed because we left without telling her, and she wants her car brought back to Miami now. She's also threatening to send me back to Puerto Rico."

"Who's Rosa?" Duke asked, looking from Stephen to Knight.

Knight heard Duke, but he ignored his boy for the moment and turned to look over at Stephen.

"What's going on with Rosa, Steph?"

Stephen switched to Spanish and opened up with the truth about how Rosa spoke with him about paying him to watch out and protect Knight, since she saw him as a great business asset, after seeing how good he was at getting rid of whatever Rosa pushed his way. She was trying her hardest to keep an eye on Knight's movement.

"So basically Rosa was using you as a bodyguard and a watchdog, huh?" Knight asked as he and Stephen held each other's eyes.

Seeing the expression on his boy's face, Duke spoke up.

"Whoa, fam! What's going on?"

"Ummm, Duke!" Ramos spoke up, pulling Duke over beside him. "I think you should stand over here beside me while the two of them handle their issue."

"Fuck that!"

"Duke!" Knight said, getting his best friend's attention, even while he stood still staring at Stephen. "Everything's cool, fam! Me and Stephen are just getting a better understanding."

Knight then turned his complete focus back to Stephen.

"So all that talk about your loyalty and devotion, was that truth or a show you were putting on?" Knight questioned Stephen in Spanish.

"I'm standing here with you not because of my auntie or even my family. I stand here because I choose to, because I want to!" Stephen confessed to Knight. "I stopped accepting money from Rosa the night I saw your loyalty and devotion to Duke after he was shot, which is why I went out of my way to find who was responsible. I've never met or had a friend like you, and I'm smart enough to know I may never meet someone like you again in this life. I know I'm not fully knowledgeable in the drug business, considering my family being who they are, but I know what my strengths are, and you are aware of them now as well. I promise on my life that nothing will happen to you as long as I breathe. Do you accept what I have to offer?"

Knight held Stephen's eyes a moment longer and honestly believed each and every word that left his mouth. Knight held out his hand to Stephen, only to receive a brotherly embrace in return.

"Ummm, excuse me!" both Knight and Stephen heard someone say as they pulled out of their embrace and looked back at Ramos.

"I couldn't help listen considering I speak Spanish as well," Ramos said jokingly. "But seriously, if there's a problem with your supplier, I just wanted to remind you both that last night I introduced Knight to Juan, who is one of the largest cocaine connects out of Cuba."

Knight remembered the arrogant and cocky Cuban and nodded his head and smirked. "I'll remember that just in case!" he said.

* * *

Knight, Stephen, and Duke finally arrived at the cookout and saw a number of guests also just arriving. Almost as soon as Knight stepped out of his SUV, he heard his name. He turned around and saw Jonathan and Cristan approaching him.

"What's up, gangster?" Jonathan said as first he and then Cristan embraced Knight.

"I'm happy you boys are here!" Knight said as both Duke and Stephen then showed love to Jonathan and Cristan as well. "By the way, I may have a job for the two of you. You fellas interested at all?"

"For the money, yeah!" Jonathan stated. "But considering who your pops is, we already know what the deal is, and we're definitely interested."

"That's what I was hoping to hear you say!" Knight replied with a smile. "Let's go talk inside."

Knight finally entered the two-story house just as Ramos was walking out of the kitchen with a drink in his hand. Knight and the others were led out into the backyard where other guests were already hanging out. He was reintroduced to a few of the people he had met at the nightclub as well as some new people who were guests of the party. Ramos also pointed out a number of business men and women who he suggested Knight should consider speaking with at some point throughout the day.

Knight broke off from Ramos after he was pulled off by a cute Spanish girl who wanted to talk to him. After excusing himself, he then found who he was looking for over by the pool smoking weed, since he could smell it in the air.

"What up, fellas?" he said as he walked up on Stephen, Duke, Cristan, and Jonathan as well as Alex and Javier, who had just arrived. "I'm glad I got all you at one time, so this should be quick."

"What's on your mind, primo?" Javier asked Knight as he passed the blunt over to him.

"Like I just told Jonathan and Cristan before you two got to the party, I've got a job for you four. I'm willing to pay each of your $10,000 a week, and depending on how well you all work, the price will rise," Knight explained.

"What's the job?" Alex spoke up.

"I've heard you four are all about your business and good at what you do," Knight started, staring at each of the killers. "I'm offering each of you jobs on the team I'm building. But I know dealing with drugs isn't really your thing, which is why I want to hire you four as my hit team. What does each of you say?"

"You already got our answer earlier!" Jonathan responded, looking back at Cristan, who nodded in agreement. "We ready when you ready."

"What about you two?" Knight asked while looking over at Alex and Javier.

"Ten grand a week!" Javier said as he smiled over at Alex before looking back toward Knight. "You got yourself some hitters, primo!"

"That's good to hear!" Knight said with a smile.

SEVENTEEN

KNIGHT MADE ROUNDS AT the cookout spending time talking with potential business associates and exchanging numbers. He paid the non-business female guests at the party very little attention since his mind was on more important things. He sat down with a Spanish woman named Maria Acosta who Ramos whispered to him was the wife of Pedro Acosta, who was currently in federal prison.

Knight spoke with Mrs. Acosta and listened to the middle-aged woman explain how she was running her husband's business but no longer had a supplier after he was sent to prison. Knight exchanged numbers with her and promised to contact her very soon.

Once the party began to slow down and guests began to leave, Knight found Ramos and pulled him off to the side.

"What's up?" Ramos asked, thinking something was wrong by the way Knight pulled him away from the guests that were still at his house.

Knight instantly waved off the worried look on Ramos's face.

"Let's ride back over to the hotel real quick. I got a little something I wanna cook up and get out on the streets. I'ma need you to take me to where I can buy a few things to cook up this shit with too."

Ramos completely understood what Knight was talking about, and he wasted no time leading him back through the house where they ran into Duke and Cristan as they were walking out to the backyard.

"Fam, what's up?" Duke asked Knight, seeing that he and Ramos were on a mission.

"We'll be right back!" Knight told him as he and Ramos continued through the house and out the front door.

* * *

Murphy and Sean stepped into Club Empire with the team after getting rid of the rest of the two bricks Knight and Duke had left them. Both of them felt as good as they looked with a pocketful of money and the team showing muthafuckers that shit was real.

Sean headed straight up to the bar area, with all eyes on them. He chilled off to the side and watched while Murphy showed off by buying bitches drinks and clowning with his niggas. Sean wasn't really feeling the whole club scene considering the shit that jumped off with the niggas K.P. and L.B. getting bodied by Knight, Duke, and crazy-ass Stephen.

Sean lost track of what he was thinking when he saw a familiar face in the club who wasn't supposed to be there—and with some other nigga, at that. Sean grabbed Murphy's arm, only to be ignored after Murphy pulled away to clown back with the boys.

"This shit is crazy!" he said while watching the bullshit that was going on a few feet from him.

Sean pulled out his phone, and within moments he took four pictures. He then sent the pictures and text messages to his boys for them to see what was really going on with their girls while they were handling business out of town.

Sean shook his head as he looked back at Karinne and April, who were all over some niggas who looked very familiar to him.

"This shit wild!"

* * *

Knight and Ramos returned to Ramos's house after they went back to the hotel and then to a store to purchase everything necessary to cook up the dope. Knight then stood up and taught Ramos how to cook dope and answered any questions he may have for him.

After cooking up the dope and allowing it to harden, he had three ounces. Knight got 10 eight balls out of each ounce for a total of 30 eight balls. He gave Ramos 3 balls out of each ounce, giving him nine in total, and pushed 7 of each ounce to the side.

"Here's what I'ma do for you," Knight told Ramos while pointing first to the eight balls. "Those right there. Do what you want with it. I don't give a fuck what, but these right here." Knight pointed to the other group of eight balls that he pushed off to the side. "Those right here, you getting off to whoever. That's a total of 30 eight balls in front of you, and all I want is $2,100 back. You think you can handle that?"

"Hell yeah!" Ramos answered, smiling as he stared down at the dope.

Knight nodded his head and saw the look on Ramos's face. He then dug out his phone when he felt it vibrate. He saw that he had received a text message and pictures. He glanced back toward Ramos and saw that his boy was already on his phone. Knight smirked before he looked back to his own phone.

Knight first opened the text message and saw that it was from Sean, Duke's cousin. He sat reading the text from Sean warning him about Karinne fucking around with some other dude. He then quickly opened up the picture and saw there were four of them.

"Oh really!" Knight said, controlling his building anger as he sat looking at the photos of both Karinne and April all over some clowns inside a club.

"Everything alright?" Ramos asked as he looked over at Knight sitting across from him at the dining room table.

"Yeah," Knight answered, even as he stood up from his seat, walked off, and called Duke's phone.

"What up, fam?"

"Fam, I'm about to send you some pictures."

"Of who?"

"Just hit me back after you check 'em out."

After hanging up with Duke, Knight sent a quick text message to Sean telling him to be on point and to expect his call in a few minutes after he handled something. He felt his phone vibrate with a reply back from Sean, just as his phone started to ring.

"Yeah!"

"Bruh, this bullshit real?" Duke asked Knight, sounding very heated.

"We're about to find out right now!" Knight told his boy as he set up a three-way call with Sean.

* * *

Sean could barely hear his phone ring, but he felt it vibrate in his hand. He stuck a finger into his left ear and placed the cell phone up to his other ear.

"What's up, big homie?"

"Who the fuck is this?" Duke barked as soon as Sean answered.

"Cuz, this is Sean!"

"Where the fuck you at?"

"Club Empire, cuz!" Sean told him. "You and big homie got my pictures I sent?"

"Sean!" Knight spoke up now. "You still see Karinne and April?"

"Yeah!" he answered. "They're actually sitting down at a table a few feet from where I'm at. But they're staring at me now! April peeped me watching them."

"Alright. This what I want you to do. Take the phone over to Karinne."

"I got you, big homie!" Sean said as he pushed away from the bar and started in Karinne and April's direction.

* * *

"Girl, he coming over here!" April said to Karinne, who was also watching Knight and Duke's boy Sean walk over to them.

"I see his ass!" Karinne said with an attitude as she sat staring hard at him.

"What up, Karinne?" Sean said as he stopped at the table at which she and April were sitting. He held out the phone to Karinne and said, "Knight wanna holla at you, shorty."

"I ain't got nothing to say to your boy!" Karinne said as she pushed the phone away from in front of her.

Sean placed the phone to his ear and reported to Knight what was said. Sean then looked at April and then handed her the phone.

"Knight wants to talk to you."

April glanced at Karinne before reaching out and taking the phone. She sighed and then placed it up to her ear. "What, Victor?"

"Bitch, what the—!"

"Duke!" Knight interrupted, cutting him off. "Fam, I got it!"

Knight heard Duke breathing hard over the line, and then called to April over the phone.

"I'm here, boy!" she answered.

"I'll make this quick since I'm aware you and your girl are having a wonderful time tonight. Since your girl doesn't want to talk, just tell her I said to give Sean the keys to the Denali and the apartment. I'm sure Duke agrees when I say to you both to do y'all, because we done! Pass the phone back to Sean!"

"Hold up!" April started.

"Bitch, pass the phone to my cousin!" Duke barked into the phone.

April sucked her teeth as she gave Sean back his phone. She then got up and walked off from the table.

"April!" Karinne yelled when she saw her girl run off.

Karinne jumped up to leave, only for Sean to grab her arm.

"I'ma need the keys to Knight's truck and apartment, shorty!" Sean told her.

"Fuck Victor!" Karinne yelled and snatched away, only for Sean to grab her arm again. "Sean, get the fuck off me, nigga!"

"Do we got a problem over here?" Sean heard someone say, looking behind him to see two older dudes walking up on him and Karinne.

"Karinne, what's up, baby?" Dollar asked, looking down at the hand that was on her arm and then looking back to her. "You know this clown?"

"Playboy, this ain't got—!"

"My man ain't talking to you, lil' nigga!" Roc spoke up as he got closer to Sean.

Sean smiled as he released Karinne and turned to face Roc.

"So this what you wanna do, huh?"

"You not even ready, lil' nigga," Roc told Sean with a murderous look on his face. "You better keep breathing and go ahead about yo' business!"

Sean peeped a few niggas that were creeping close and watching, so he nodded his head before looking over at Karinne.

"Shorty, you already know what it is now. I'ma let Knight handle it from here. You took it here!"

* * *

Dollar had heard the name for at least the tenth time since arriving in Miami. He stood watching the young hustler walk off while talking on a cell phone. Dollar then looked back at Karinne and saw that she was also watching the young dude.

"Who's dude, Karinne?"

"He's a friend of my ex-boyfriend," she told him. "I'll be back, Dollar. I gotta use the restroom."

Dollar watched Karinne until she disappeared into the crowd. He then looked back at Roc and wasn't surprised to find his right-hand man watching him.

"You heard the name again too, huh?"

"Of course," Roc answered. "You think he's really the one behind K.P.'s murder?"

"From what we've heard so far, he's one of the three main names said to be responsible. So until we find out just who really killed my brother, we'll keep an eye on everyone that's involved."

EIGHTEEN

AFTER THE BULLSHIT OF discovering Karinne and April playing games, Knight gave instructions to Sean to keep an eye out on the homeboy with whom he had gotten into it. Sean and Murphy then visited Orlando for their re-up and to drop off Rosa's Audi in Miami where the agreed upon spot was, with the money for the ten bricks. Knight was no longer worried about the money since he was already making things happen in Kissimmee with Ramos, who was getting rid of work and making new connections with buyers who were introduced to him. Knight spent the next few days reaching out and building his business all over the city of Kissimmee, even setting up shop with different hustlers that needed a new supplier. He also let his hit team—of Jonathan, Javier, Alex, and Cristan—loose on a mission to deal with a problem that Mrs. Acosta was having.

The three young men moved out of Gaylord Palms Resort into a mini-mansion inside a gated community named Poinciana. It was a luxurious four-bedroom suite house with an additional suite designed as a private guest quarters with its own kitchen and private entrance. Knight, Stephen, and Duke each had their own bedroom suite.

Knight returned home after having a meeting with his new

Cuban connect, Juan, with whom he decided to work after discussing it with Donavon. They felt it was time to move on to a different connect, and Juan had better prices for his product. Knight walked into his bedroom just as his cell phone went off in his pocket.

"What up, fam?" Knight said, after seeing Duke calling and answering the phone.

"Well, damn! You sure know how to keep a promise to a girl, Victor McKnight!"

Slowly smiling after recognizing the voice, Knight said, "Explain to me why you're with my brother, Kia?"

"You sound jealous, Knight! Are you jealous, handsome?"

"Answer the question, woman!" he demanded, even though he was still smiling.

"If you must know, I ran into Duke at the hotel. He was with someone, and I stopped him to ask about you since you up and left and never called me back."

"My apologies, but I've been really busy, ma!"

"How about making it up to me and coming to see me?"

"You still offering to braid my hair? I do want it taken care of."

"Come to the hotel, and I'll meet you out front. What are you driving?"

"Benz G-Wagen."

"Well damn! I see you've really been busy. Hurry up, handsome."

After hearing the line die, Knight could only chuckle thinking about her.

* * *

Kia heard her cell phone begin to ring while standing in the lobby at Gaylord Palm talking with her co-worker and friend Tamara. Kia dug out her phone from her Chanel bag and smiled when she saw who was calling.

"Girl, hold on! This is my future husband calling," Kia told her girl. "Hey, handsome. Where are you?"

"Come outside, ma!"

Kia motioned for her girl to follow her outside, and told Knight she was on her way. She hung up the phone and walked toward the front entrance.

"Where's this man at?" Tamara asked as she followed Kia out of the hotel. "I gotta see this one, because the last one I wasn't impressed with."

Kia rolled her eyes at her friend, just as the sound of a car horn was blown. Kia looked ahead and spotted the Mercedes-Benz G-Wagen that was slowly pulling up and stopping right in front of them. She watched as Knight stepped out of the SUV and walked around to the passenger side.

"Oh my God!" Tamara said, staring at the guy with his hair in a ponytail who was now walking toward her friend. "Kia, he is gorgeous, girl!"

Kia smiled after hearing her girl's comment, and then she accepted the single, red, long-stem rose Knight held out for her. She smiled even harder after also accepting the kiss to the cheek he gave her.

"Hey, gorgeous!" Knight said, smiling as he gently ran the back of his hand down along her smooth and soft skin. "You miss me, ma?"

"Yes!" Kia admitted before she realized what she was saying, really unable to focus with Knight touching her and the smell of his cologne in her nose. "Ummm, Knight. This is my friend Tamara!"

"Tamara!" Knight repeated, shifting his gaze over to the friend as he took Kia's hand and intertwined their fingers. "It's good meeting you, but if it's okay, can I have Kia for a few hours?"

"Enjoy!" Tamara said, smiling at Kia as Knight led her away to his Benz.

He opened the door for her and then helped her inside by effortlessly lifting her from her feet by her small waist and setting her into the passenger seat.

"You good, beautiful?"

"Yes, I'm good, Knight," she replied, smiling as she watched him after he shut the door for her and then walked around to the driver's side and climbed in.

"You hungry, ma?" Knight asked, glancing over at Kia as he was pulling off from in front of the hotel.

"Not right now," she answered while staring at him. "Knight, what's going on?"

"What do you mean, ma?" Knight asked as he glanced over at her.

"Don't 'what do you mean' me, Knight!" Kia joked. "What's up with this new attitude you've got?"

"I don't know what you're talking about, ma!" he replied, giving her a little wink and a smile.

* * *

Knight made a stop and picked up a pizza and chicken wings from the pizza shop Ramos had told him about. He then pulled up to the security gate at the community entrance and drove through until he pulled up in front of his place and turned down the drive.

"Knight, who lives here?" Kia asked as she stared out of her window at the mini-mansion.

"I do!" Knight replied as he pulled around the back of the mansion and then hit the remote for the garage door.

"Excuse me?" Kia asked, staring at him as he pulled inside. "You live here?"

"Yeah, I'm renting while I'm in Kissimmee," he explained after shutting off the G-Wagen. "Come on!"

After Kia climbed out of the SUV, she noticed another Mercedes-Benz parked to the right. She simply shook her head not understanding who Knight really was. She followed him through the garage and through a door that led into a big kitchen, where she saw a middle-aged Spanish woman cleaning up what looked like a spotless kitchen.

"Carmen!" Knight addressed the live-in servant. "This is a friend of mine, Kia Johnson."

Kia spoke with the women for a moment, and then Knight led her by the hand from the kitchen and up some steps.

"Knight, you really stay here, don't you?"

"Yeah! Why?" he asked as he led Kia through the upstairs hallway and into a full movie theater.

"What in the world!" Kia cried in surprise and shock. "Boy, you have a movie theater in this place, too?"

"Pretty much!" Knight stated as he handed Kia the food. "You got something special you wanna watch while we eat?"

"It doesn't matter, Knight," Kia told him as he was walking off.

After Knight disappeared and left Kia alone, she looked around the theater just as the lights suddenly lowered. Knight reappeared a few minutes later carrying a six-pack of Heineken and a six-pack of bottled water.

"There's a rolling table against the wall," Knight told Kia, pointing to the table to her left.

Once the two of them were set up to eat and relaxing inside the theater-style seats, Kia saw the name of the movie they were about to watch: *All Eyez on Me*.

"I was meaning to see this movie when it came out!" she said with a smile.

"Now you can see it with me!" Knight said as he handed Kia a plate with a slice of pizza on it.

"Thank you!" Kia said.

She sat back and just stared at Knight for a few moments. She was very surprised at how strongly she was attracted to him.

* * *

After *All Eyez on Me* was over, a second movie began. Knight sat on the floor between Kia's legs getting his hair braided up, when his phone went off from inside his pocket. He dug out the phone to see that Mrs. Acosta was calling.

"Yeah!" Knight answered.

Kia listened to Knight's side of the phone conversation and easily figured out that he was talking with a woman, since she could hear her clear enough to know it was a female voice. Kia felt a sting of jealousy watching Knight smile and speak in Spanish with whoever the bitch was on the other end of the line.

"So when are you going to teach me how to speak Spanish?" Kia asked Knight as he hung up his phone.

"Why?" Knight asked as he looked back over his shoulder at Kia. "You trying to follow my phone calls now?"

"Excuse me?" Kia responded loudly while giving Knight a look. "What would I need to follow your conversation for? Why would I even care what you talk about with other women, Knight?"

"Whoever said it was a woman?" Knight asked with a smirk back at Kia. "But real talk, beautiful. That was a business call with a customer of mine."

"Customer?"

"Yeah!"

"Boy, what type of business you running that you got customers, living in a mansion, and driving a Benz G-Wagen?"

"Let's just say that I give the people what they want!"

"Okay, I get it!" Kia stated with a smile. "You sell drugs, huh?"

Knight didn't bother to answer her. He simply turned around and leaned back to allow her to continue what she was doing. He remained quiet a few moments and was just about to ask a question, only for Kia to beat him to it.

"So how's things with you and your girlfriend?" Kia asked as she continued braiding his soft, long hair.

"My who?" Knight answered. "That's been over with for about a week or two now."

"What happened?" she asked, paying full attention now after hearing that he was no longer with Karinne.

Knight waved his hand dismissively and changed the conversation.

"So what's up with you? What dude I gotta take you from?"

"What makes you think I'm looking to be taken?" Kia asked

with a small smile showing while her heart was beating faster and harder.

"So we playing like that now, huh?" Knight wanted to know as he looked back at her again over his shoulder. "You gonna sit there and act like there ain't nothing between us?"

"Us?"

"That's what I said!" Knight said as he turned to face Kia up on his knees. "What's up with us, ma?"

"What do you want to be up with us, Knight?" Kia asked as she stared into his eyes.

Knight caught the way Kia's eyes lowered to his lips before quickly returning to meet his eyes.

"Come here, ma!" he told her with a smile as he gently grabbed the back of her neck and pulled her toward him as he leaned forward to meet her lips in a kiss.

Kia shut her eyes and accepted Knight's tongue as she returned the kiss. She then wrapped her arms around his neck as their kiss deepened. She felt Knight lift her up and gently lay her down onto the carpet. She gave a soft moan as his body lay between her legs and against her body.

"Knight! Baby, wait!" Kia told him, feeling Knight's hand undoing her jeans.

"Yeah, ma! What's wrong?" he asked, lifting up from Kia a little bit and looking down to meet her eyes.

"Knight, I can't lie! Baby, I've wanted you since I first saw you; but if we take things to this level, this has to be the end type of thing. I don't plan on letting you go once I have you, and can't no nigga get this pussy or my heart once I give it to you!"

"That's all I needed to hear!" Knight replied, smiling before bending down and returning to kissing her as he went back to undoing her jeans.

NINETEEN

KNIGHT WAS FLOODING ALL of Kissimmee and most of St. Cloud with the new shipment of fifty keys of cocaine about a month after switching connects from Rosa to Juan. Although he received threats from Rosa, his new dealings with Juan were bringing in $17,000 a key. He ran into a few problems that were instantly dealt with while business kept moving forward and the team continued growing. Knight continued to find new buyers and wanted to expand faster.

That night he and Kia were lying in bed laughing at Adam Sandler's *Water Boy*, which was playing on the wall-unit television in front of their bed. Knight picked up his cell phone after hearing it ring.

"Yeah!"

"Knight, it's Melody."

"Melody, what's up?" Knight asked while peeping Kia shooting a questioning look at him, which he ignored.

"Knight, Donavon told me to tell you it's time!"

Knight sat up in the bed after what Melody had just told him. He asked no questions but simply said, "Give me a few days and I'ma be back in Miami. I gotta make sure things out here are in order. But I'ma need you to find a new spot for me and my lady. Don't trip about the price, shorty!"

"I'll take care of it for you, but Donavon wants you to come and see him as soon as you get back."

"Everything good with Pops?" Knight questioned with worry.

"He will explain when you get back, Knight."

"I'll call when I'm already on the road!" he told her as he hung up the phone and climbed out of bed.

"Knight, baby, what's going on?" Kia asked.

"Ma, we leaving!" Knight told her as he walked into the bathroom with the phone up to his ear.

* * *

Knight made numerous calls and met with his people to let each of them know what was going on, explaining that until told otherwise they would contact Ramos whenever business was concerned. Ramos would then contact him. He also gave orders to Duke to get with the street hustlers that were working for the team or buying work from them.

Knight got a few of the workers to help Kia with getting together whatever it was that she was taking with her, after the two of them had a talk about her leaving her job and life that she had made for herself in Kissimmee. He also got with his hit team and let Jonathan and the others know that they were leaving for Miami. He received no complaints from any of his killers, who were actually hyped and ready for the road trip.

Once everything was in place by the third night after he had received Melody's initial call, Knight, Duke, Stephen, the hit team, and two of his street soldiers were ready to leave Kissimmee early on Friday morning.

* * *

"Are you ready to tell me what's going?" Kia asked her man as she sat in the passenger seat of his Benz G-Wagen as they drove back to Miami with a trail of four cars and a brand-new 2018 Ford F350 Excursion Platinum Edition.

"Kia, remember what I told you once before?" Knight asked before repeating himself. "Some things are better you don't know."

"Knight, do not feed me that bullshit, nigga!" she told him, since she was beginning to get upset. "I've completely given up everything I've worked for, all at your request to leave Kissimmee with you to return to Miami. You're going to tell me something!"

Knight remained quiet a few moments until Kia said his name in a tone that got him to cut his eyes over to her. He chuckled and then shook his head.

"I left Miami after something happened, but now my pops wants me to come back. It sounds like there's another problem."

"What happened before that you had to leave Miami?" she asked.

"That, you don't need to know!" Knight told her and then switched the subject. "Once we get settled in, you can start looking into finding a building to open up your salon."

Kia rolled her eyes at Knight at how he just blankly ignored what they were talking about as if it wasn't even important. Kia dug out her phone to call her girl Tamara, to check exactly when she was coming to Miami since they agreed to open up their hair salon business.

* * *

"Hello!" Melody said into her phone after answering it as she and her baby Cam'ron sat watching the television together.

"Melody, I'm outside, shorty!"

Immediately recognizing Knight's voice and hearing him hang up, she looked at Cam'ron.

"Little man! Knight's here!"

"Where?" Cam'ron asked, looking up at Melody with an excited expression on his face.

"He's outside!" Melody told him, smiling when she saw the look on his face. "Come on!"

Both of them jumped up from the sofa and ran to the front door. They walked outside to the parking lot and easily spotted the Mercedes-Benz G-Wagen that Knight and his two friends were standing and talking in front of.

"Knight!" Cam'ron yelled as he took off running toward him.

When Knight heard his name, he turned around and broke out in a smile when he saw his little man. Cam'ron slammed into Knight and hugged him when he reached him.

"What's up, lil' man? You miss me, huh?"

"Of course," Cam'ron said, causing Knight and the others to burst out laughing.

"That's my lil' man!" Knight said as he wrapped his arms around him before looking back to smile and meet up with Melody's eyes. "What's up, lady?"

"Hey, Knight!" Melody said, still smiling as she walked over and hugged him around the neck, followed by a kiss on the cheek.

She stepped back to look him over.

"You look really good!"

"And I'm still jealous Donavon found you first!" Knight replied, which caused Melody to smile harder. "You got everything set up for us?"

"Of course!" Melody replied. "I'll ride with you because we need to talk and Donavon wants us both to come see him!"

"Well, you and lil' man go get ready and we out of here!" Knight told her, smiling as he stood watching both Melody and Cam'ron walk back into the apartment complex.

"Ummm, excuse me, Knight!" Kia said, drawing not only his attention with her tone, but the attention of Stephen and Duke as well. "Who exactly was that?"

"Kia, relax, ma!" Knight told her, after seeing the look on her face, which he was becoming too familiar whenever she got jealous.

"That's my pops's lady."

"Whose son is that?" Kia then asked, remembering how the young boy reacted to seeing Knight.

"He's my son!" Knight answered, just as he heard Cam'ron calling.

Knight looked back to see his little man jump from the sidewalk and rush out to him, with Melody trailing behind him.

* * *

Knight left Melody's apartment complex and followed her directions out to Miami Beach. He pulled up in front of a double gate that allowed entrance onto the grounds of the mini-mansion. Knight used the passcode Melody had given him to open the gate, and he then pulled the G-Wagen through. He continued up the circular drive and parked in front of the custom-furnished courtyard.

"Knight, please tell me this isn't another mansion you own?" Kia asked, after climbing from the Benz and looking around at the estate grounds.

Knight didn't bother to answer Kia; instead, he followed Melody through the front gate and into an outdoor foyer, with Cam'ron right beside him. Knight continued following Melody after she unlocked the front door and they all entered.

"Oh my God!" Kia cried in amazement at how beautiful it looked inside.

"Where'd you find this?" Knight asked Melody, with an

impressed look on his face.

"You're renting this place from a friend I met through Donavon," Melody explained as she took his hand and said, "Come on! Let me show you around the place."

"Lead the way, shorty!" Knight said, smiling as he, Cam'ron, and Melody walked off farther into the mansion, unaware of how Kia was staring at them.

* * *

Melody gave Knight the full tour of the 4,000 square-foot four-bedroom, three-and-a-half-bath mansion that also had a den. She then took him outside and showed him the lanai with the large pool, spa, and outdoor kitchen with lush landscaping. There were even two private guesthouses.

"What do you think, Knight?" Melody asked, smiling at him as they stood next to the swimming pool.

"I think you did your thing, shorty!" Knight told Melody as he dropped his arm around her shoulders.

"Well, you can have the place as long as you want. It's already taken care of with the money you sent to me," Melody informed as she held onto Knight's waist only to hear someone loudly clear her throat just as Kia appeared.

"Knight, we need to talk!" Kia told him with an attitude.

Knight stared down at his Gucci watch and then released Melody and turned to Kia.

"Ma, can it wait until I get back? I've gotta go visit my pops real quick."

Knight didn't bother to wait for Kia's reply. Instead, he called for Melody and Cam'ron and then walked back into the house, again unaware of Kia simply staring at him.

* * *

Karinne smiled as soon as her father entered the visitation booth. She kept her eyes locked on her father until he sat down on the edge of the table. She then picked up the phone just as he was picking up the phone on his side.

"Hi, Daddy!"

"You actually remembered you had one in jail, huh?"

Karinne lowered her eyes in embarrassment since she knew she was dead wrong for not visiting her father in almost two months.

"Daddy, I'm sorry. I was just upset because I felt like you sided with Victor over me," she said softly.

"Karinne, if you would have listened, you would have learned that Knight was only doing as I told him."

"Why couldn't you just tell me where he was? He was my boyfriend, and I had a right to know, Daddy."

"You don't need to know everything, Karinne," Donavon told his daughter. "Knight was only following my orders to leave for a while."

"Why?"

"You do not need—!" Donavon paused in the middle of what he was saying once his eyes locked on the young man that stepped off the elevator.

Donavon immediately broke out in a smile at the sight.

Seeing her father's smile and attention were elsewhere, Karinne turned to look in the direction he was staring. She froze once her eyes met the person that was only a few feet from her.

"Victor!"

Knight was surprised to see Karinne but said nothing to her other than to nod his head in greeting. He looked at Donavon and nodded to his father and mentor, to which he received a nod right back.

Karinne looked back at her father and heard herself ask, "What's he doing here, Daddy?"

"I called him back home!" Donavon told his daughter. "Don't leave. Put Knight on the phone."

Karinne sucked her teeth as she tossed the phone down and stood up. She gave Knight some space, not wanting to be close to him right now since she was having mixed feelings.

Knight heard Donavon knock on the glass, so he picked up the phone.

"What up, Pops?"

"What's going on, Son?" Donavon stated, still smiling as he looked over his boy. "You look real good, youngin. I see you've even cut your hair."

"No time to really take care of it, so I cut it!" Knight explained. "So how you holding up in there, old man?"

"It's what it is, Don! But I start trial soon."

"How's everything looking?"

"That's why I called you back home, Knight. I've had the attorney checking out a few things, and I found out who the snitch was who told the cops on me. I found out where the muthafucker lays his head at and all."

"Say no more!" Knight told him.

He was ready to murder whoever was responsible for his father being locked up.

"Tell me the address, and it's done!"

Donavon nodded his head upon hearing and fully understanding what his son was telling him.

"I'll give you the address, but there's a way I need you to handle this. I really think this is bigger because I know this person very well; and there has to be a real good reason why he switched out on me, when I actually thought he was a solid brother," Donavon explained.

"However you want it, it's done, Pops!" Knight promised Donavon.

And Knight intended to keep his word by any means necessary.

TWENTY

KNIGHT WALKED OUT OF the jail after his and Melody's visit with Donavon, where he received the information that was necessary to help his father get released and be freed from the case being held over his head. Knight heard his name being yelled, but he continued escorting Melody and Cam'ron over to his SUV.

"Victor!" Karinne yelled again, catching up to Knight, grabbing his arm, and snatching him around. "I know you hear me calling your ass!"

Knight stared into Karinne's eyes and then turned around again.

He handed Melody the keys to his G-Wagen and said, "Wait for me in the truck."

Knight watched as Melody and Cam'ron did as he asked, and then he turned back around to face Karinne.

"What?"

"Excuse me?" she asked with much attitude. "That's all you got to say to me?"

"Truthfully, you're lucky to get that out of me!" Knight told her. "You either going to say what you wanna say or I'ma continue what I was doing. Leaving!"

"So that's how you treat me now, huh?" she asked, causing Knight to laugh out loud, which only made her even more pissed off. "What the hell you find so damn funny?"

"You!" Knight answered with a smile. "There's a lot you don't get, but you will in a few days. But do me a favor. Let your boy Dollar know that since he's been looking for me, I'm back and now I'm looking for him!"

"What's that supposed to mean?" Karinne asked him, after grabbing Knight's arm as he turned to leave.

Karinne met his eyes again and just stared a few brief moments.

"I'll tell you this, Karinne. You remember the night Duke was shot? Well, we found the person responsible, and I found out that bullet was meant for me!"

"What does that have to do with Dollar, Victor?"

"Because the guy who was found with his head separated from his body, that was your man Dollar's young brother. That's why he's been looking for me!"

Karinne stared open-mouthed at Knight as he walked off and headed to his SUV. He unlocked the doors, and then Melody and Cam'ron climbed inside.

What Knight had just told her was all Karinne could think about.

"Oh God!"

* * *

Karinne rushed straight over to April's house after leaving the jail, only to find Gina there. She got her girls together in April's bedroom.

"Girl, what the hell is wrong with you?" April asked, after seeing the look on Karinne's face and how she was acting.

"Y'all not going to believe who the hell I just saw earlier!" Karinne told her girls, not giving them any time to respond. "Victor is back! His ass showed up at the jail to see my father."

"You lying!" April asked.

"Girl, no!" Karinne cried. "His ass showed up with that bitch who's been keeping Cam'ron, and then he got the nerve to be acting like he got an attitude with me."

"Karinne, you did cheat on that boy!" Gina reminded her, to which she was rewarded with looks from both her girls—which she paid no attention to.

"Anyways!" Karinne began, rolling her eyes at Gina. "You all are not going to believe what Victor told me!"

"So you actually did talk to him then?" April asked with an attitude. "What did he say about Duke's ass?"

"We ain't talk about Duke!" Karinne yelled. "But we did talk about Dollar though."

"What?" both April and Gina cried out together.

Karinne explained to her girls what Knight had told her about Dollar and his brother, and what plans Knight had for him.

"Girl, what are you going to do? You know what type of team Dollar and Roc rolling with; and even though Victor got Stephen and Duke and the cousins, what's five guys against Dollar's forty guys?" April expressed with concern.

"Sean and Murphy got a team they built since Victor was away!" Gina explained.

"Girl, that lil' boy shit ain't enough!" April said as she shot Gina a look.

"I'ma talk to Victor!" Karinne spoke up, getting both girls' attention. "His ass pissed me the fuck off, but I still love his ass, and I'ma still have his back. I gotta warn him about Dollar before he gets himself killed."

"How are you going to reach him?" April asked. "Did you get his number too?"

"No!" Karinne answered. "But when it comes to Victor, my father is serious about him; and if I talk to my father, I believe I can get Victor's phone number so I can talk to him."

"My question is, do you think Victor will actually listen to what you have to say?" Gina asked as she stared hard at Karinne.

Karinne was worried about the same thing. She sat on her spot on April's bed wondering if she could actually get Knight to listen to her, so she could warn him about what he was getting into.

* * *

Knight met up with his team at the hotel at which they were staying until they got settled in, renting out the whole top floor of the Hilton on Miami Beach. Knight met with Duke, Stephen, and the hit team to discuss what their next move was going to be.

"So, we making a trip up to New Jersey?" Duke asked after Knight was finished talking to the group.

"Trenton, New Jersey!" Knight specified.

"This Russell dude. How you wanna deal with homeboy, primo?" Javier asked Knight.

"From what I've been told, he's got a team around him. But I'ma let you and Jonathan handle the team. I just want Russell brought back to me alive!"

"When are we leaving?" Cristan asked next.

"Tonight!" Knight answered, just as his phone woke up.

He dug out his iPhone from his pocket to see that Kia was calling.

Knight excused himself from the team and entered another room to answer the phone.

"Yeah, Kia. What's up, ma?"

"Knight, where are you? You've been gone for hours and left me in this big-ass house all by myself. Where the hell are you?"

"My fault, baby," Knight apologized. "Ma, I told you before we left Kissimmee that it's always business until I can get my pops out of jail."

"So why tell me to come to Miami if you don't have time for me . . . for us?"

"Kia. Look, baby! I just need a few days to get things straightened out, and I promise I'll spend time with you. Right now, though, I need to handle something important!"

"What about me?"

Knight remained quiet for a few moments and came up with an idea.

"I tell you what, ma! I'ma send a car over to you, and you'll have two of my boys with you to go and pick up your girls, Tamara and Keisha. Bring them back to Miami with you, and I'll have one of my debit cards with them. Matter of fact, I'ma leave both debit cards for you. There's $5,000 on each card. That should hold you until I get back."

"Where are you going, Knight?"

"I'll explain when I get back," he told her. "The two dudes coming with the car are Trevor and Paul."

"Whatever, Knight!"

Knight heard Kia hang up in his face, but he could only shake his head. His phone rang again, and he saw that it was Melody calling.

"What up, Melody?"

"Knight! Donavon and Karinne are on the phone for you."

"Who's on the—?"

"Youngin, relax!" Donavon interrupted Knight before he got started.

"What up, Pops?" Knight said after sighing loudly.

"I want you to talk to Karinne," Donavon explained, but paused a few moments when Knight remained silent. "Remember the incident that led to you having to leave for a while?"

"Yeah! What about it?" Knight asked.

"Baby girl," Donavon called to Karinne.

"Yes, Daddy!" Karinne answered.

"Knight's right there. Talk to him!" Donavon told her. "You two talk like you both got some damn sense!"

"Victor!" Karinne called.

"Yeah!"

"Victor, look, we really need to talk!"

"I'm listening."

"Not on the phone. In person, Victor."

Knight remained quiet a few moments and then spoke up. "Meet me at your mom's house, and we can talk before I leave town."

Knight then called to Donavon and Melody and asked, "Pops, you got anything else? Melody, you got something?"

"We'll talk once you get back, son!" Donavon told him.

"We also need to talk, Knight, but it can wait until you get back from taking care of whatever you need to do."

"Alright," Knight replied before hanging up the phone.

* * *

Karinne got Gina and April to go with her to her mother's house. When they arrived, she was surprised to see Eric and her mother's man talking out at Eric's truck. Karinne parked her new M5 BMW in the driveway beside her mother's car.

"What's Eric doing here?" April asked, looking back at both Eric and Karinne's mother's soon-to-be husband.

"I don't know, and do I care?" Karinne answered as she and her girls got out of the car.

"Yo, Karinne!"

Karinne heard Eric call out to her, but she ignored him and continued walking toward the front door, only for Eric to run up on her and grab her arm to stop her.

"Get the fuck off me, nigga!" Karinne yelled as she snatched away from him.

"Karinne, relax!" Eric told her, holding up both his hands in surrender. "I just wanna talk to you real quick."

"What the hell do you have to say that I want to hear, nigga?" Karinne asked with attitude as she placed both hands on her hips.

"Karinne, I know I fucked up bad!"

"Karinne, girl, look!" April interrupted Eric as she pointed out to the street.

Karinne looked past Eric to see the Benz G-Wagen she instantly recognized in the lead, followed by a black matte Aston Martin DB9 and black metallic Chevy Camaro SS. Karinne stood staring as the G-Wagen slowed to a stop, the passenger door opened, and Knight climbed out.

"Oh my God!" April cried out in shock at the sight of Knight.

"He cut his hair for real, Karinne!"

Karinne heard April, but she was too busy staring at Knight as he walked into the yard and past her mother's man. He then made his way to where Karinne stood with her girls. She was fully aware of her heart beating hard and fast in her chest.

"I'm here!" Knight stated as he stopped in front of Karinne. "Let's talk!"

"Hold up!" Eric called out as he stepped between Karinne and Knight, only to freeze up when his eyes locked in on not only the G-Wagen, but also the Aston Martin and Camaro.

Eric next saw the doors open and out step Duke and four guys with guns in their hands.

"Oh shit!" April and Gina said in unison, after seeing what had just happened.

Knight slowly smirked when he saw the expression on Eric's face when he saw what was behind him.

"How 'bout you just leave now!" Knight ordered Eric.

Karinne watched as Eric did as he was told, before she looked back toward Knight and met his eyes.

"Let's get this over with. I've got something to take care of!"

* * *

Karinne sat on her bed while Knight leaned against the wall across from her.

"Why'd you cut your hair?" Karinne asked first.

"What is it you gotta talk about, Karinne?" Knight asked, ignoring her question.

"So that's how it is now, Victor?" she questioned. "You can't talk to me without acting like that?"

"Acting like what, Karinne?"

"Like you don't even care about me anymore!"

"What?" Knight answered with a laugh at what she just said. "You gotta be joking! You the one fucking the same muthafucker that wants to kill me and driving the shit he bought yo' ass. Where you living now, Karinne?"

Knight waited a few moments for her to answer the question. He smiled when she had nothing to say.

"You ain't gotta answer me. I know you living with that nigga already; and it's cool, because that just shows me where you stood all along!"

"Fuck you, Victor!" Karinne yelled as she got up into his face. "Nigga, you will not blame this on me! If you would have treated me like your woman, some other nigga wouldn't have got the pussy!"

Karinne jumped back after seeing how red-hot angry Knight became. She realized what she said and started to say something else, only to end up grabbing his arm to stop him from leaving the bedroom, which caused him to snatch away.

"Victor, please!" Karinne cried as she wrapped her arms around him from the back and held on to him. "I'm so sorry, baby! Victor, I love you, and I know I really messed up. But I still love you!"

Knight was quiet after hearing Karinne's confession before he finally spoke up.

"Let me go, Karinne. I gotta go, ma!"

"Just listen to me, please!" she told him as she got in front of Knight and met his eyes.

"Baby, I need to tell you about Dollar. He has a big team of guys that's backing him, and he has this guy named—!"

"Roc!" Knight finished her words.

He then wiped the tears away from her face.

"I know all about this dude and his team. I was having him watched, which is how I know about you and him living together."

"Victor, I'm sorry!" Karinne cried again as she wrapped her arms back around him.

She laid her head against his chest and cried softly.

"Baby, I want you back in my life, Victor! I'll do whatever you ask of me if we can be together again. You promised me that I wouldn't want for nothing as long as you still breathe. Well, I want you! Give me what I want!"

"I can't right now!" Knight admitted.

Karinne leaned back to look into Knight's eyes and said, "What do you mean?"

"I mean I'm seeing someone now, Karinne!" he confessed.

Karinne released Knight and stepped back to get a better look at him.

"Who is she?"

"Her name's Kia!" he told her. "She's from where I just left."

"So you plan on going back to her then?" Karinne questioned, folding her arms across her chest.

"I don't have to. She's here with me!" Knight told her.

"Send her ass back where she came from! You're my man, Victor! Or do you want to be with her?" Karinne said in response.

Knight shook his head and sighed. "Kay, let's talk about this once I get back, okay! I gotta go and take care of this shit for Donavon!"

"Give me a kiss!" she told him, grabbing Knight by the front of his shirt and pulling him toward her.

Their lips met in a kiss that quickly turned passionate. She moaned as he pulled her harder up against him while gripping her butt with both his hands.

* * *

"Well it's about time!" Mrs. King said with a smile when she spotted her daughter and Knight together.

"Hey, Mrs. King," Knight said, smiling as he kissed her on the cheek, before turning back toward Karinne. "I'ma see you when I get back, ma!"

"Be careful!" Karinne begged him. "I love you!"

"Yeah!" Knight replied, winking his eye at her before he started to walk off. He then paused and turned around. "I love you too, Kay!"

Karinne smiled as she stood watching Knight walk out to his Benz G-Wagen. She called out to April, who refused to let go of Duke.

"Girl, let that man go handle his business. They coming back!"

To be continued . . .

Text Good2Go at 31996 to receive new release updates via text message.

To order books, please fill out the order form below:

To order films please go to ***www.good2gofilms.com***

Name:____

Address:____

City: ______________ State: ______ Zip Code: ___________________________________

Phone:____

Email:____

Method of Payment: Check VISA MASTERCARD

Credit Card#:____

Name as it appears on card: ____

Signature: ____

Item Name	Price	Qty	Amount
48 Hours to Die – Silk White	$14.99		
A Hustler's Dream - Ernest Morris	$14.99		
A Hustler's Dream 2 - Ernest Morris	$14.99		
A Thug's Devotion	$14.99		
Black Reign – Ernest Morris	$14.99		
Bloody Mayhem Down South	$14.99		
Business Is Business – Silk White	$14.99		
Business Is Business 2 – Silk White	$14.99		
Business Is Business 3 – Silk White	$14.99		
Childhood Sweethearts – Jacob Spears	$14.99		
Childhood Sweethearts 2 – Jacob Spears	$14.99		
Childhood Sweethearts 3 - Jacob Spears	$14.99		
Childhood Sweethearts 4 - Jacob Spears	$14.99		
Connected To The Plug – Dwan Marquis Williams	$14.99		
Connected To The Plug 2 – Dwan Marquis Williams	$14.99		
Connected To The Plug 3 – Dwan Williams	$14.99		
Deadly Reunion – Ernest Morris	$14.99		
Flipping Numbers – Ernest Morris	$14.99		
Flipping Numbers 2 – Ernest Morris	$14.99		
He Loves Me, He Loves You Not - Mychea	$14.99		
He Loves Me, He Loves You Not 2 - Mychea	$14.99		
He Loves Me, He Loves You Not 3 - Mychea	$14.99		
He Loves Me, He Loves You Not 4 – Mychea	$14.99		
He Loves Me, He Loves You Not 5 – Mychea	$14.99		
Lord of My Land – Jay Morrison	$14.99		
Lost and Turned Out – Ernest Morris	$14.99		
Married To Da Streets – Silk White	$14.99		

M.E.R.C. - Make Every Rep Count Health and Fitness	$14.99		
Money Make Me Cum – Ernest Morris	$14.99		
My Besties – Asia Hill	$14.99		
My Besties 2 – Asia Hill	$14.99		
My Besties 3 – Asia Hill	$14.99		
My Besties 4 – Asia Hill	$14.99		
My Boyfriend's Wife - Mychea	$14.99		
My Boyfriend's Wife 2 – Mychea	$14.99		
My Brothers Envy – J. L. Rose	$14.99		
My Brothers Envy 2 – J. L. Rose	$14.99		
Naughty Housewives – Ernest Morris	$14.99		
Naughty Housewives 2 – Ernest Morris	$14.99		
Naughty Housewives 3 – Ernest Morris	$14.99		
Naughty Housewives 4 – Ernest Morris	$14.99		
Never Be The Same – Silk White	$14.99		
Stranded – Silk White	$14.99		
Slumped – Jason Brent	$14.99		
Someone's Gonna Get It – Mychea	$14.99		
Supreme & Justice – Ernest Morris	$14.99		
Supreme & Justice 2 – Ernest Morris	$14.99		
Supreme & Justice 3 – Ernest Morris	$14.99		
Tears of a Hustler - Silk White	$14.99		
Tears of a Hustler 2 - Silk White	$14.99		
Tears of a Hustler 3 - Silk White	$14.99		
Tears of a Hustler 4- Silk White	$14.99		
Tears of a Hustler 5 – Silk White	$14.99		
Tears of a Hustler 6 – Silk White	$14.99		
The Panty Ripper - Reality Way	$14.99		
The Panty Ripper 3 – Reality Way	$14.99		
The Solution – Jay Morrison	$14.99		
The Teflon Queen – Silk White	$14.99		
The Teflon Queen 2 – Silk White	$14.99		
The Teflon Queen 3 – Silk White	$14.99		
The Teflon Queen 4 – Silk White	$14.99		

The Teflon Queen 5 – Silk White	$14.99		
The Teflon Queen 6 - Silk White	$14.99		
The Vacation – Silk White	$14.99		
Tied To A Boss - J.L. Rose	$14.99		
Tied To A Boss 2 - J.L. Rose	$14.99		
Tied To A Boss 3 - J.L. Rose	$14.99		
Tied To A Boss 4 - J.L. Rose	$14.99		
Tied To A Boss 5 - J.L. Rose	$14.99		
Time Is Money - Silk White	$14.99		
Two Mask One Heart – Jacob Spears and Trayvon Jackson	$14.99		
Two Mask One Heart 2 – Jacob Spears and Trayvon Jackson	$14.99		
Two Mask One Heart 3 – Jacob Spears and Trayvon Jackson	$14.99		
Wrong Place Wrong Time – Silk White	$14.99		
Young Goonz – Reality Way	$14.99		
Subtotal:			
Tax:			
Shipping (Free) U.S. Media Mail:			
Total:			

Make Checks Payable To:
Good2Go Publishing
7311 W Glass Lane,
Laveen, AZ 85339

CPSIA information can be obtained
at www.ICGtesting.com
Printed in the USA
LVHW01s1933120618
580546LV00011B/617/P

9 781947 340121